Praise for *Attack of the Kill*

"In "Attack of the Killer Tumbleweeds," Antonia Rachel Ward shows her skill in blending genre and emotion into one fantastic package. With the glamorous setting of Las Vegas, Ward constructs a glitzy tale of couples caught up in a mysterious threat that might be out of this world. Ward combines fantastic characters with poignant storytelling and a delightful cinematic feel that will make the reader experience the story as though they were watching it on the big screen at a retro theater. Absolutely not one to be missed."
—Zachary Rosenberg, author of *Hungers as Old as this Land*

"Attack of the Killer Tumbleweeds is pure, unadulterated B-movie bliss. With additional stories in the form of a Western bloodbath and creepy carnival slasher, Ward's dark fiction continues to reinforce her growing reputation as a true, and gifted, storyteller."
—Stephanie Ellis, author of *Reborn* and *The Five Turns of the Wheel*

"Wild, fast and full of the thorns! Attack of the Killer Tumbleweeds is a thrill ride you won't soon forget. Perfect for fans of old school B movies."
—Joshua Robinson, author of *The Devil's Gift* and *Before the Rising Sun*

"Ward's Attack of the Killer Tumbleweeds gives you exactly what you want from that sort of title: an absurdly entertaining B-movie premise situated in a garish setting full of larger-than-life characters. But don't get lost in the glitz and glam of the Vegas backdrop, because underneath it all is a charm and heart that truly brings the story to life."
— Alex Ebenstein, author of *Curse Corvus* and *Melon Head Mayhem*

ATTACK OF THE KILLER TUMBLEWEEDS

AND OTHER STORIES

ANTONIA RACHEL WARD

Attack of the Killer Tumbleweeds!

For horror movie lovers everywhere

CONTENTS

ATTACK OF THE KILLER TUMBLEWEEDS!

1

Nevada, 1958.

Somewhere in the desert ...

Jimmy had brought the gun but forgotten the cannoli. *Damn.* He ran his finger over the grip of the revolver that lay on his knee, hidden by the darkness in the back of the car. A job like this took a lot out of him. He liked to have a little something sweet for afterwards, to steady his nerves.

He caught Luca's eye in the rearview and gave him the slightest nod. It was time. Dessert or no dessert, the job needed doing.

The third guy in the car was Paulo, and he was dead. He

just didn't know it yet.

He sat in the passenger seat next to Luca, yammering on about some girl in Vegas he had his eye on. He liked her. Was thinking of asking her for a date. But he was dead. Jimmy was about to make sure of that.

Luca slowed the car. A lone tumbleweed drifted across the desert road, glinting silver in the headlights.

Jimmy lifted his gun. Paulo didn't notice a thing.

"… and Glitter—she's a showgirl—she says she's a friend of Dean Valentine. You know Dean, don'tcha, Jim? Hey, why're we stopping? I—"

Paulo fell silent.

"Get out the car, Paulo," Jimmy said.

"Hey, guys …" Paulo scrabbled for the door handle. "We can talk about this …"

"Nobody wants to hear you beg." Jimmy lifted his gun, aiming it at the back of Paulo's neck. "Out. I don't want your brains on my upholstery."

Paulo turned to the driver. "Luca. We're friends, right? You know I wouldn't … I never … I ain't no snitch!"

Luca sniffed and stared straight ahead. The engine idled. Jimmy sighed, pushed away thoughts of the cleaning bill as he squeezed the trigger, felt the familiar resistance as it started to give way.

Crack.

The sound split the night, loud enough to damn near burst Jimmy's eardrums, and with it came a blinding flash of light. There was a thud. The car shook. Windows rattled. Jimmy flinched, squeezing his eyes shut, and the bullet went through the roof.

Luca grunted. Jimmy opened his eyes, a ghostly, saucer-shaped after-image dancing across his vision. Through it he saw the shadowy figure of Paulo scramble out the door and fall to his knees in the dust.

"The heck was that?"

Paulo's voice sounded fuzzy beneath the ringing in Jimmy's ears. They were under fire. The Japanese had spotted their convoy and—

Jimmy shook himself, gripping his gun. All was silent in the desert, apart from the sound of Paulo scrambling to his feet. There were no Japanese. The war was over. They were in Nevada, miles from anywhere. Nobody could be after them: nobody even knew they were here.

"Damn." Jimmy fumbled for the handle of his own door and shoved it open, ready to go after that chicken shit. He'd chase him down if he had to. The son of a bitch wouldn't get far out here.

But Paulo wasn't running. He wasn't moving at all. He just stood there, haloed in the headlights, staring straight ahead.

Jimmy lifted his gun to the back of Paulo's head. Then he saw what Paulo was looking at.

An eerie, silverish glow pulsed from a crater a few feet from the road. It thrummed with energy—a low, rumbling hum that Jimmy felt rather than heard. It seemed to call to him, and he found himself wanting to walk towards it, into its star-like embrace.

Slowly, he lowered his gun.

A car door slammed, and Jimmy flinched again. He almost ducked, expecting gunfire, or shells flying overhead. Then Luca shuffled over to stand beside him, and the moment passed.

"What is it?" Luca asked, in his slow, dumb way, turning over the mystery like a cow chewing cud.

"Damned if I know." Jimmy didn't look away from the glow. What was down in that crater? Whatever it was, it had shot across the sky and crashed there—a plane, maybe? *Damn.* A plane meant a pilot, and a survivor meant a potential witness. Jimmy couldn't risk that.

"Keep an eye on him," he told Luca, indicating the mesmerized Paulo with an incline of his head. "I'm gonna check it out."

But before he could make a move, a tumbleweed danced across the desert floor and dropped into the crater. The silver light flickered, and a moment later the tumbleweed re-emerged, followed by another just the same. And another. And another. Ten, twenty, thirty of them, and more, poured out of the crater like a wave.

They advanced on Jimmy and his associates like an enemy platoon, flowing over each other. The eerie silver glow lit them from behind, turning them shadowy and menacing.

Jimmy's hands shook. His gun was slippery in his palm. Backing away, he fired off shot after shot, but it made no difference. The tumbleweeds piled themselves high, towering over the three mobsters in a wall that must've been fifteen feet tall. They paused there, wobbling, and Jimmy got the creeping sense that he was being watched. Assessed. He knew enemy behavior when he saw it.

"This ain't right," he muttered. "This ain't right."

"Forget this." Paulo's voice trembled. "Let's get outta here."

He turned, took a step toward the car. And the tumbleweeds descended. The wall crumbled; the weeds spilled over Paulo, knocking him flat on his stomach, blocking him completely from sight.

Paulo's screams sliced through the night air. Agonizing screams. The kind of screams Jimmy hadn't heard since his time in the Philippines.

Jimmy froze, heart racing, torn between his instinct to fight, and his desire—growing stronger—to flee. He watched as Luca whipped out his gun and fired useless shots into the tumbleweeds. They barely seemed to notice—if clumps of dead plant could be said to *notice* anything. Yet Jimmy was sure he could sense them thinking, turning their attention to Luca, registering him as a possible threat. Yes, that was it. He was a threat to them. And Jimmy—Jimmy had already fired at them once.

As Paulo's howls died away, the weeds whipped round and descended upon Luca. Jimmy didn't wait to see what they'd do to him. He bolted. Ran past the bleeding, shredded remains of Paulo. Jumped into the car and gunned the engine. As he slammed his foot onto the gas and skidded away, Luca's cries faded into the distance. The plants filled the rearview, tumbling after him as he sped back to Las Vegas. Jimmy gripped the steering wheel and put his foot to the floor, refusing to slow up until he saw the glittering lights of the city within reach.

He was going to need that goddamn cannoli.

2

The neon peacock towered high above Cindy-Lou's head. She craned her neck for a better look, colors splashing across her face in the darkness. Blue. Green. Purple. Gold.

"Say, would you just look at that, Buddy!" she cried, pointing up at the sign. "It looks as though its tail is moving. Do you see?"

"Sure I do." Smiling, Buddy slipped an arm around his new wife's shoulders. "It's mighty fine."

Alongside the bird, flashing green letters spelled out the name of the Peacock Hotel, and below it, a sign announced the show for that night: *Dean Valentine and the Fabulous Tiki Girls*.

"Stay right there." Buddy stepped back and raised the camera that hung around his neck.

Beneath the glowing sign, Cindy-Lou brushed down her skirt and struck a pose that she hoped would look glamorous, one hand on her hip, smiling as the flash went off.

"I can't believe you arranged this for our honeymoon,"

she said, when he was done taking photographs. "Dean Valentine! I'm so happy I could burst!"

Buddy chuckled. "How about you wait until after the show before you do that? You don't want to miss anything."

She laughed and thumped him playfully on the arm. "You think you're such a wit."

"Maybe I'll get myself a slot on the bill."

"With your singing voice? I heard you in the shower this morning. You'd clear the place out in no time."

"Hey! Isn't a wife supposed to support her man in whatever he wants to do?"

"I'm just being honest," Cindy-Lou replied with a sly grin. "What's a relationship worth if you can't be honest?"

"You're lucky I love you, that's all I'm saying." Buddy kissed the top of her head, then turned to pull their bags from the trunk. A bellhop in a dapper green uniform hurried over to help, following with the luggage as the newlyweds headed through the big glass doors with their monogrammed 'PH' handles.

In the hotel lobby, a huge golden peacock statue shimmered atop a carpet of swirling colors. Cindy-Lou paused to admire it while Buddy checked them into their room. Then they headed upstairs to change for dinner.

Cindy-Lou put on a lemon-yellow cocktail dress, while Buddy sported the same suit he'd worn for their wedding just days before: cream, with a red bow tie. She couldn't help but gaze at him with pride and amazement. What with the way his blue eyes crinkled when he smiled, he reminded her of Steve McQueen. To think this handsome man was her *husband*. How fine it sounded. She'd enjoyed listening to Buddy introduce her to the concierge as 'Mrs. Hitchcock'. It had an awful nice ring to it.

"You ready?"

"Just a moment." Cindy-Lou leaned close to the mirror, circling her mouth with red lipstick before checking the pins in her dark hair. "Okay. Let's go."

The Peacock's famous Tiki Lounge was already full of impossibly glamorous patrons, chatting and sipping drinks beneath a canopy of false rainforest foliage. A troupe of dancers swayed their hips on stage, wearing sequin-spangled bikinis and feather headdresses—the Fabulous Tiki Girls the sign had advertised.

Cindy-Lou clutched Buddy's arm as they wove their way through the white-clothed tables, looking for their seat. As they reached their table, the waiter pulled out a chair for her, and Cindy-Lou sat down, sweeping her petticoats aside.

"We're so near the stage!" she exclaimed.

Buddy beamed. "Best seats in the house."

"Oh, Buddy Bear. I know you feel bad that we couldn't go to Hawaii, but this is just *wonderful*. I really couldn't ask for more."

Dinner arrived. The lights dimmed. Cindy-Lou turned to the stage, hardly remembering to take a bite of her steak as the hotel manager announced the next act: Dean Valentine. She put down her fork and joined in the applause, giddy with excitement, as the man himself strode into the spotlight.

Dean Valentine! The face from the movies. He looked just like the poster on the wall of Cindy-Lou's childhood bedroom—the bedroom she had, in fact, only recently vacated. Tanned with a chiseled jaw, his dark hair swept back in a relaxed quiff, he wore his lounge suit with the kind of casual insouciance that would have invited a caustic comment from Cindy-Lou's God-fearing mother. And as for her father … well, the old preacher had some awful theories about how Dean Valentine had gotten his first job in the movies, which Cindy-Lou refused to give any credence to. Every time Valentine showed up on the television, her father would shut it off, muttering something about mobsters.

But when Dean sang, how could anybody imagine he'd needed anything other than his own talent? His voice was a velvet purr, his smile dazzling white. Cindy-Lou couldn't take her eyes off him the whole time he was on stage. He sang all her favorites: 'Heartbreaker', ''Neath an Italian Moon' … and for the encore, his biggest hit, 'Driftin''.

When he finally left and the dancing girls returned, she felt as though she'd just emerged from a long fever dream.

"How did you like that?" Buddy asked.

"Oh, he's wonderful, isn't he?"

"Well, how'd you like to meet him?"

"*Meet* him?" Cindy-Lou's eyes widened, then she shook her head, half-laughing. "Why, that'll never happen."

"It will if we have backstage passes." Buddy pulled two cards from his pocket, and Cindy-Lou stared at them in astonishment.

"My goodness, did you …? Are we really going backstage?"

"Right after the show." Buddy sat back, folding his arms with a satisfied smile. "Now, come on, you'd better eat your dessert before they take it away."

3

Glitter knew the newlywed was gonna cause trouble the moment the girl walked into the dressing room. With her dark hair swept up in a ponytail, and her big, innocent blue eyes, she looked barely out of high school. She stopped just inside the doorway, clutching her purse in front of her with white-gloved hands, staring at Dean like a deer caught in head-lights.

The husband, following behind her with a hand on the small of her back, was stocky-shouldered like a farm-boy. With his doughy complexion and his buzz-cut, he didn't stand a chance against Dean, who still had his Hollywood glaze, even if it was a bit chipped at the edges these days.

Glitter turned to her dressing table to unpin her feather headdress from her peroxide-blonde hair. She watched through the mirror as Dean hoisted himself out of his arm-chair and set his glass of Scotch on Glitter's dressing table, before slouching over to shake the husband's hand.

"Dean Valentine. How'd you do?"

"Buddy Hitchcock," said the farm-boy. "And this here's my wife, Cindy-Lou."

"It's an honor, ma'am." Dean took her hand and bent to kiss it. Cindy-Lou started giggling uncontrollably.

"Don't let him charm you." Glitter put down her head-dress and faced them. "He's a real heartbreaker."

Cindy-Lou giggled some more. 'Heartbreaker' was one of Dean's most popular hits, and the joke always landed well with fans. *If you can't beat 'em, join 'em* was Glitter's motto. It wasn't like she and Dean were a pair of high-school sweethearts, 'going steady'. They were adults. They took things easy. And maybe that meant she couldn't stop him from playing around, but she *could* make herself part of the act.

"I saw you onstage!" Cindy-Lou turned her attention to Glitter. "You're a fine dancer, if you don't mind my saying so."

"I better be," Glitter replied. "Been doing the same show for over a decade. Name's Glitter, by the way. Say, you folks want a drink?" She headed for Dean's drinks cabinet. "We got whiskey, vodka ..."

"Oh, I don't drink hard liquor," Cindy-Lou said. "I'll have a soda, if you don't mind."

Soda. Glitter poured her a gin and tonic and popped a little umbrella in it to soften the blow.

"This is Vegas, baby doll. We don't do temperance."

Cindy-Lou smiled politely and took a dainty sip—so dainty it made Glitter want to slap her. She resisted the urge and poured a whiskey, which she handed to Buddy, and a dirty martini for herself.

"Take a seat." Dean sat back down in his armchair, indicating the sofa opposite. With his dinner jacket still on, collar open, he slipped easily back into the cool cat guise he wore on stage. Buddy and Cindy-Lou settled themselves—Cindy-Lou perching on the edge of her seat with her hands in her lap—while Dean lit a cigar.

"Smoke?" he asked, offering one to Buddy.

"No, thank you, sir." Buddy sounded like a schoolboy trying to impress his girlfriend's father.

"Just got married, hey? And you thought you'd come to Vegas to celebrate?"

"Yes, sir. We don't live far off, y' see. We were hoping to go to Hawaii, but I have to work."

"Well, I'm glad you came to see the show instead. I can stand to be second choice." Dean took a slow drag on his cigar. Glitter rolled her eyes.

"Oh, but you're not second choice!" Cindy-Lou cried, predictably. "I'm just so darn excited to be here, Mr. Valentine. I own all your records, and I've seen all your movies. *Mississippi Belles* is my favorite."

The way she looked at Dean, you'd have thought he was some kind of saint, and not a washed-up forty-something trying to sleaze his way through the tattered remains of his career. Besides, under that red velvet lounge suit, he was getting a bit of a paunch. Unfortunately, there were always girls like Cindy-Lou ready to persuade him he hadn't quite lost his touch.

Glitter plucked an olive from her Martini and sucked on it, catching Buddy's eye.

"What's it you do?" she asked him. "Must be pretty important if you couldn't even take time off for your honeymoon."

"I'd love to tell you, ma'am," Buddy replied, "but sadly, I cannot. It's classified."

"Classified! My, my." Glitter sashayed past the couple, the beads on her bikini jangling, and took a seat on Buddy's other side, squashing up close to him on the sofa. "Why all the secrecy? Say … you don't work at the military base, do you? The one out past Indian Springs? No, I guess you can't answer that, either. But one of the girls was talking about it the other day. I heard there're all kinds of strange goings on over there."

"All hearsay, ma'am." Buddy's farm-boy charm faded, replaced by the closed expression of someone who knew better than to show his hand. Glitter had grown up around poker players—she knew the look well.

"Well, I won't press you." She patted him on the thigh. "You folks staying in the hotel?"

"We sure are. Just arrived today."

"Hey, Glitz, why don't you take Buddy on the backstage tour?" Dean said, as though the idea had only just occurred to him. "Sure he'd love to meet the other girls, wouldn't you, Bud?" He gave Buddy a wink.

Buddy and Cindy-Lou shared a glance.

"If it's all right with you, sir, I'll just stay here," said Buddy.

"Oh, don't stay on account of me," Cindy-Lou cut in, biting her lip. "If you'd rather go …?"

Glitter knew her role. She downed her Martini and stood, holding out her hand to Buddy.

"Come with me. The girls sure will be thrilled to meet a fan, won't they, Dean?"

"They sure will."

"Come on." Glitter tugged at his arm until he stood and hustled him towards the door. When she glanced back, Dean hadn't taken his eyes off Cindy-Lou.

Glitter led Buddy through the back of the theater, passing

racks overflowing with sequined costumes and hunks of painted set-dressing. He seemed morose and kept glancing over his shoulder.

"Say, can't we just go back?" he asked. "I don't like to leave Cindy-Lou alone."

"She's not alone," Glitter said. "I'm sure she and Dean are having a real nice chat. Here," she steered him towards a nearby fire exit, "why don't we step outside? The strip is real pretty at night."

She opened the door, and the heat hit them, the air still dry as cinders even after dark. Glitter led the way along the block to the Peacock Hotel's main entrance, where the neon bird flashed its tail above the parking lot. Her hip clicked now and then as she walked, an irritating reminder that it was only a matter of time until her high-kicking days were over, and she would be relegated to working the craps tables on the casino floor.

"You got a cigarette?" She stopped on the corner beneath the blinking Peacock sign, ignoring the tourists who approached to snap Polaroids of her in costume.

"Sure." Buddy patted his pockets until he found a pack of Marlboros and lit one for her, then one for himself. For a while they smoked in silence, gazing at the lights that sparkled all down the strip. A stray tumbleweed drifted past their feet.

Glitter looked around, wondering how to break the silence.

"See that? That's Dean's Cadillac," she said at last, indicating a sea-green convertible parked close to the front door. "Nice, ain't it?"

"Sure is." Buddy barely glanced at the car. He took a drag of his cigarette, then added, "I really ought to get back to Cindy-Lou. It's late."

"She'll be fine for a few more minutes." Glitter slipped her arm through Buddy's. "I thought we could get to know one another a little, you know?"

Buddy stiffened. "Ma'am, I'm flattered, but you already know I'm married."

"And you're in Vegas! Relax. Enjoy yourself." She leaned in, lowering her voice. "Besides, we're just talking, ain't we?"

"I—I guess ..." Buddy glanced back at the hotel again.

"Your wife'll be fine. Dean knows how to take good care of her. Tell me ..." Glitter hunted her mind for a topic of conversation. "What's it like working at that military base? What do y'all really do there?"

"It's like I said, ma'am. It's ..."

"Classified, I know." Glitter pressed up against his arm. "I won't tell anyone, I promise."

"Well ..." Buddy looked down at her, seeming to assess

the likelihood of her getting him into any kind of trouble. "It's actually been pretty exciting lately. I wish I could tell someone about it. I'm not even allowed to tell Cindy-Lou. She thinks I'm designing rockets for NASA."

"But you ain't?" Glitter probed.

"Not exactly. Not at all, in fact." He took another drag of his cigarette, frowning. "But I can't talk about that. Hey, why don't you tell me something about yourself? You got a real name? Can't imagine you were christened Glitter."

Glitter laughed. "Not that I'd remember it, but I'm pretty sure I wasn't christened at all. So Glitter will do, for now."

"All right then. You worked in this hotel long?"

"Long as I can remember, just about. My mom was a cocktail waitress in the Lounge. My dad was a patron, you know how it is." She glanced at him, then laughed. "Naw, you don't know how it is. Bet you grew up in a place with a white picket fence and two dogs. Bet your wife was the girl next door, am I right?"

Buddy laughed. "I guess so. I knew Cindy-Lou from school. She was the Homecoming Queen." He smiled wistfully. "Never thought in a million years someone like her would look twice at a square like me, but hey, just goes to show, don't it? If you don't bet, you'll never win."

"Well, if you're a betting man, you're in the right place."

"That's the crazy thing. I never was, 'till I bet on her. All in. Knew she was the one, ever since sixth grade. Took me till after we graduated to work up the courage to ask her on a date, though."

He chuckled, then suddenly his expression darkened, as if a thought had just occurred to him. He finished his cigarette, ground it out beneath his shoe, and turned to the hotel.

"I'm gonna head back in, Miss Glitter. I'm sorry to say, but your friend Mr. Valentine gives me a real uneasy feeling. You'll have to excuse me."

He dropped Glitter's arm and strode across the parking lot, heading for the main entrance. Glitter watched him while she smoked the tail end of her cigarette. He was a handsome boy. Naïve, but sweet along with it. She almost felt guilty about the shock he was about to receive. But hey, he would have to encounter the real world sometime. Why not now?

4

"Are you sure we're allowed to be out here at this time of night?"

Cindy-Lou stood in the Peacock's central courtyard, looking out over the silent swimming pool. Lights from the surrounding hotel rooms glittered on the water's surface, and the voices of guests in the nearby cocktail bar were a muffled clamor. Dean Valentine stood beside her, holding two bright red drinks topped with fruit and umbrellas.

"Allowed?" He chuckled, handing her one of the glasses. "You're a worrier, aren't you, Popsicle?"

Cindy-Lou smiled shyly. "I suppose." She took a tiny sip of her drink, to be polite. It tasted strong and sweet. "I really oughta go find Buddy, though."

"I'm sure your old man is having a fine time with Glitter and the other girls."

The image of Buddy surrounded by scantily clad chorus girls flashed through Cindy-Lou's mind. Perhaps her father had been right about Vegas. *Sin and temptation.*

Dean took a seat on a nearby sun lounger and patted the space beside him. "Sit down, take a load off."

Cindy-Lou hesitated, feeling foolish. If she sat right beside him, they'd be awful close together. Say Buddy came back and saw them—he mightn't like it. But if she didn't, Dean might think she was rude. After a moment's hesitation, she came to a compromise and took a seat on the lounger opposite. Dean scooted his closer so their knees almost touched.

Close up, she saw the fine lines around his eyes, could even smell the scent of cigar smoke coming off him. *Dean Valentine.* She'd daydreamed about this moment many times, gazing at his picture on the front of her favorite record; humming along to the words of *Driftin'.*

You and me girl / We're just tumbleweeds driftin' in the breeze.

There'd been times—bad times, before she'd even started seeing Buddy—when Dean's music had felt like her only solace. Her parents hadn't approved, of course, but she hadn't always been the good preacher's daughter they'd dreamed of. Then she'd taken up with Buddy—*such a nice boy*—and things had settled themselves into a pattern that made sense. A route to her future that felt well-trodden, easy to follow. Marriage. House. Dog. Kids. All she had to do was follow the road signs. Well … up to a point.

Dean Valentine had been there, in a way, through her darkest hours. A comfort. A friend, of sorts. And now he was sitting right opposite her. Her stomach fluttered. She sipped her cocktail slowly, but the sweet alcohol did nothing to settle her nerves.

"You're a fan of *Mississippi Belles,* huh?" Dean asked.

"Sure am!" Cindy-Lou let out a nervous laugh. "Always thought Lavinia Taylor was the most beautiful girl I ever saw."

Dean leaned forward. "Sure, she's pretty. But she's not a patch on you." He reached out to brush a stray strand of hair away from her face. His touch was rough. Sandpapery. Cindy-Lou's heart beat wildly. How many times had she pictured a moment just like this? She never would've imagined it would happen in real life.

She looked into Dean's deep blue eyes, intensely aware of every fine detail of his face. The crinkled lines across his forehead. The crooked nose, thick lips.

The next thing she knew, those lips were touching hers.

Cindy-Lou jumped up, pushing her lounger back. Her drink fell from her shaking hands and spilled across the ground. Chunks of fruit scattered over Dean's highly polished shoes.

"Mr. Valentine!" she cried. "I'm married!"

"Now, now." Dean got to his feet. "No need to make a

fuss …"

Cindy-Lou slapped him in the face. It was like hitting a block of wood. Dean didn't flinch, only raised his eyebrows as she picked up her purse and wrapped her shawl around her shoulders.

"If you'll excuse me," she said in the firmest voice she could muster, "I'm going to find my husband."

5

Buddy was close to the hotel entrance by the time Glitter finished her cigarette and decided to hurry after him. In the end, she couldn't face letting the poor guy stumble upon his wife with Dean—not without some warning, at least.

The performance of splitting up a visiting couple was one Dean and Glitter had played out countless times. Dean didn't go for single women—he assumed they were desperate, that they were after his money, that they would pressure him into marriage, get pregnant, leave him with even more alimony bills. He was two wives down already, and he couldn't afford that sort of mistake. So a married woman, staying in the hotel for a short while, was perfect prey for him. One as young and naïve as Cindy-Lou would be doubly tempting. And if the newlywed was only going to be around for a couple days, Dean wasn't about to waste any time.

Glitter went along with it because it was going to happen with or without her help. She preferred to be in on the trick, rather than one of the people getting played. And on those nights where there were no Cindy-Lous around, when the hotel was quiet and the weather was cool—on those nights, she was the one who was there for Dean. His best friend. His confidante.

She supposed it was better than nothing.

"Hey, Buddy, wait up." She almost tripped in her haste to stop him from entering the hotel. She was trying to protect the husband, she told herself, not Dean. Dean deserved everything he got.

Buddy paused in front of the revolving doors. Glitter ran to him and grabbed his arm, laughing and gazing up at him in that way guys usually liked.

"You're not going to abandon me already, are you? Say, how'd you fancy a walk down the strip? Just you and me?" She pouted. Batted her eyelashes. Saw in Buddy's firm expression that she was wasting her time.

"I gotta get back to Cindy-Lou."

Here was a man who was genuinely in love with his wife. Why, she oughta put him on the market and sell him—a rare breed like that would fetch her a pretty penny.

Glitter was about to give up when she heard the screech of tires. She and Buddy turned to see a black Ford careering down the strip. It veered into the wrong lane, and horns blared from the cars coming the other way.

"Goddamn drunk drivers," Buddy muttered.

Glitter shrugged. "Happens all the time."

But this driver was worse than most. The Ford swerved a Greyhound, spun across the road, and bounced over the sidewalk, slamming straight into the Peacock's neon sign. The bonnet crumpled, and the engine began to smoke. A worried crowd gathered, gawping beneath the lights that flickered and burst.

Before Glitter even had the chance to open her mouth, Buddy jogged across the parking lot.

"What are you doing?" she called after him.

"I'm going to see if anybody needs help!"

He was already at the driver's door when it flew open, and a man in a pinstripe suit staggered out. He reeled around, almost falling, and swiped a fedora from inside the car, jamming it onto his head, before turning to stare, wild-eyed, at Glitter and Buddy. Blood trickled down the side of his face.

"Jimmy?" Glitter grimaced. This wasn't good. This wasn't good at all.

Jimmy squinted at her. "Glitter? Dean's girl?"

"Is there anyone else in the car?" Buddy leaned around Jimmy to get a better look.

"Only me," said Jimmy. He was paler than Glitter had ever seen him. "I went out with Luca and Paulo but they—

ANTONIA RACHEL WARD

they're gone."

As he spoke, he glanced back down the strip, his voice wavering, and discomfort settled into Glitter's bones. Something about this situation didn't feel good. Jimmy 'the Shark' Catalano was one of Dean's oldest friends: a war veteran, and a hardened gangster. Who had he been driving away from in such a hurry?

"Let me just have a word with my friend," she told Jimmy. She took hold of Buddy's arm and pulled him a few feet away, out of earshot. "We gotta go. You don't know who this guy is. This is Jimmy the Shark. Whatever's got him rattled like that can't be good."

Buddy frowned. "Could be he's in shock. We ought to take him to a hospital."

"Leave him!" Possibilities raced through Glitter's mind, edging her close to panic as she thought of the kind of people Jimmy might've angered. "You don't understand. Somebody could be coming after him, and we don't want to be here when they arrive."

"Glitter." Jimmy stumbled over to them, holding a handkerchief to his bleeding temple. "Glitter, you gotta listen to me."

"No," said Glitter. "I don't got to listen to anything."

"Paulo's dead," Jimmy went on, his eyes wide. "He died."

Glitter wondered whether he'd been taking something. She frowned. "People die in your line of work all the time, Jim. You know that better'n anybody."

"No. No. No. This wasn't like normal. Not like normal. It came from the sky. I saw it. And *they* came out of it. The t-t-tumbleweeds. And they killed him. Paulo. And Luca too. The tumbleweeds killed them both." He squinted down the road, breathing hard. "They're coming. I can't see 'em, but they're coming."

Something twisted in Glitter's guts.

"This don't seem right at all," she muttered to Buddy. "Please, let's just go."

But Buddy frowned, interested. "What is it you saw, Jimmy?" he asked. "Can you describe it?"

Jimmy shook his head, as though trying to clear his thoughts. "Round. Silver. I can't—they're coming!" He gripped Buddy's lapels. "You gotta listen to me."

"All right. Calm down."

"Don't you tell me to calm down!" Fury boiled up behind Jimmy's eyes. He thrust his face into Buddy's, baring his white teeth. "I'm tryna tell you something important, so don't you tell me to calm down!"

Buddy gave him a firm shove, and Jimmy stumbled back. Incensed, he hurled himself at Buddy, slamming him against the car. Buddy tried to regain some ground, but

Jimmy held him fast with one hand, reaching into his pocket with the other. Glitter saw something flash in his palm.

"Buddy, watch out! He's got a knife!"

Buddy managed to duck Jimmy's swipe, but barely, and as he tried to regain his balance, Jimmy took the upper hand again, jabbing at him with a mad look in his eyes. Buddy dodged, but he looked out of his depth—he was big, and Jimmy was fast.

Then, *bang!* Somewhere in the street a car backfired, and Jimmy froze, startled. Buddy seized his moment and rallied with a firm right-hook. Jimmy crashed to the ground.

"Goddamn." Glitter peered down at him, then up at Buddy. "You punched his lights out."

"High school boxing." Buddy put his hands on his knees while he caught his breath. "Comes in handy now and then."

"Thought you said you were a square."

"That was *why* I boxed in high school."

Glitter stared down at Jimmy. Blood trickled from his already crooked nose.

"You've made a big mistake," she whispered. "He's gonna be mad when he wakes up."

"He seemed unhinged. We should take him to a hospital."

"No." Glitter shook her head firmly. "No, you don't understand. We're in big trouble now. First we get out of here.

Then we go talk to Dean. He'll know what to do."

..*.*.*.*.*.*.*.

Glitter and Buddy hurried through the hotel's main entrance. The lobby was almost empty: one receptionist stood at the gold-topped desk in her neat green suit, while a few late arrivals jostled for her attention. Glitter ducked her head as she passed them, trying not to be noticed despite her beaded bikini and feathers. For once in her life, she wished not to be memorable. If they were lucky, Jimmy was so drunk or stoned that he wouldn't remember a thing by the time he woke up.

"Hey," she heard the receptionist say, "did somebody just crash into our sign? I heard a commotion."

She was squinting out the window at the parking lot, her face crumpled into a frown.

"It was nothing." Glitter tried to sound airy and unconcerned. "Just some drunkard."

She slipped through the staff-only door into an empty corridor, Buddy following her through the rabbit warren of hallways back to Dean's dressing room. When they found it empty, Buddy's expression clouded.

"Where d'you suppose they went?" he asked, frowning.

Glitter sighed. Having just seen Buddy lay out Jimmy,

she wasn't sure she fancied Dean's chances if he got caught in a clinch with Cindy-Lou. Still, they needed to talk to him, preferably before Jimmy woke and regained his bearings.

"I'm sure I can guess," she said, turning back the way they'd come.

The pool was Dean's favorite place to take prospective conquests. She knew, because that was where he'd taken *her,* one evening years ago, when she was as young and foolish as Cindy-Lou.

There'd been something about the stillness of the water at night—the dim glow of the lights; the hum of the cicadas—that made it the most romantic place in the hotel after dark. Even though she'd known the hotel inside out by then, Glitter had still been captivated—more by Dean than the location, it was true. He'd bought her a drink, and sat with her on a sun-lounger, and told her she was prettier than Lavinia Taylor. Glitter had fallen for it hook, line, and sinker.

The worst part was that she still felt a pang of longing when she thought about it, even now. Because even though he was a sleaze and a playboy, she knew all that was just a front. She'd seen him in his vulnerable moments, drunk, late at night. Crying about the fact that his record sales were slipping; that he never saw his kids anymore. Worrying about dying old, alone, and forgotten in some grimy motel room. And all Glitter could do was listen and wonder why there was still this invisible barrier between them that meant he would drop her the moment some fresh face came on the scene.

She led Buddy through the bar and out to the poolside, bracing herself for fireworks. But no sooner had they stepped out the door than they met Cindy-Lou coming the other way. Her cheeks were pink, her expression indignant.

"Buddy!" She threw herself into her husband's arms and buried her face in his shoulder. "I'm so glad you're here."

Buddy stepped back, holding his wife at arm's length to examine her face. "Is everything all right? Say, nobody's upset you, have they?"

Cindy-Lou glanced over her shoulder at Dean, who stood sheepishly by the sun loungers in a puddle of strawberry daiquiri and fruit. He looked so pathetic with his hands stuffed in his pockets and his head bowed that Glitter had to stifle a laugh.

"No," said Cindy-Lou, after a moment's deliberation. "Nobody's upset me. I'm just relieved to see you. I didn't know where you'd gotten to."

Dean kicked a slice of kiwi off his shoe and approached them. "What's going on, Glitz?"

"We got a problem, Dean. A real problem." Glitter flung herself down on one of the loungers and slipped off her high heels, massaging her tired feet.

"Well, tell Uncle Deano all about it." Dean took a seat beside her and placed his hand between her shoulder blades, massaging the base of her neck.

As the newlyweds settled on the lounger opposite, Glitter explained about their encounter with Jimmy, ending with a sigh, "… and then Buddy knocked his lights out."

Dean took his pack of cigarettes from his pocket and lit one, his expression serious. "Where's Jimmy now?"

"Last I saw, he was KOed on the sidewalk."

"You left him there?"

"What was I supposed to do?" Glitter protested. "This is Jimmy we're talking about. If we were still there when he came round, he'd probably be pulling out Buddy's teeth by now."

"I wanted to take him to the hospital," Buddy cut in, glancing at Cindy-Lou. "It wasn't right to just leave him there."

"He'll be fine. Hungover, sure. Mad, too. But he'll live. Gimme that." Glitter took the cigarette from Dean's fingers and availed herself of a long drag to settle her nerves. "Question is, how do we manage him when he comes looking for us?"

"Is this man a real mobster?" Cindy-Lou said, her eyes round as saucers.

"Real as you or me," Dean replied. "But he's nothing for

you to concern yourself about, trust me."

"He's one of the worst." Glitter ignored Buddy shaking his head at her. She didn't give a damn whether Cindy-Lou was frightened. She oughta be. "Real nasty piece of work. D'you think they call him Jimmy the Shark because of his fantastic dental work?"

"And he's gonna come for Buddy?" Cindy-Lou clutched her husband's hand. "Well, what are we going to do? Should we leave? We could drive back home tonight, Bud."

"There's no need for that," Dean said. "You folks enjoy your vacation. I'll check on Jimmy in the morning and explain there's been a misunderstanding, that's all. He's a close personal friend of mine. He'll understand." He shot Cindy-Lou his best, most dazzling Hollywood smile. "Don't you worry your pretty head about a thing, Popsicle."

6

Later that night, after the newlyweds had retired to their hotel room, Glitter stood at the window of Dean's penthouse suite. Behind her, Dean snored loudly in the king-sized bed, wrapped in black satin sheets. An empty whiskey bottle and an overflowing ashtray sat discarded on his nightstand.

It was past one in the morning, but the lights along the strip still flashed as bright as ever. Cars came and went, and every so often there was a burst of chatter and laughter from partygoers making their way back to the hotel. No matter what time it was, the lights were always on in Vegas. Glitter liked that. There was always something to do, somebody to talk to. You never had to be lonely in this city.

Except when you were.

She lit herself a cigarette, the flame from her silver lighter flaring in the darkness, and thought about Buddy and Cindy-Lou. They had so much ahead of them, and Glitter couldn't help feeling a pang of envy as she imagined their future. No doubt they'd settle down in some idyllic little town with a park, and a white-painted church, and a Mom-and-Pop grocery store. Buddy would go out every day to work while Cindy-Lou looked after the babies—a few of them, probably. She seemed the maternal type. There would be birthday parties and ball games and all the things Glitter never had. All the things she *would* never have.

Bitterness caught in the back of her throat. Maybe she ought to take a leaf out of Dean's book and seduce Buddy. Sure, he loved his wife, but he'd cave eventually. They all did … unless she was losing her touch. She supposed it had to happen someday. At thirty-five, her career as a dancer was almost over, and what else did she have to look forward to? A lifetime of dealing cards and dishing out cocktails? And Dean … as long as he didn't drink himself to death.

Glitter squinted. There was some kinda commotion going on way down the strip. A few cars had stopped in the middle of the street, their drivers gathering in the road to point and shout. What were they all making such a fuss about? Cupping her hands against the glass, she peered closer. Looked like … tumbleweeds? A pile of tumbleweeds blocking the road. A strong wind must've blown them in from the desert. It wasn't unheard of.

From the bed, Dean snorted and rolled over. Glitter sighed. Perhaps a drink would help her sleep. A little nightcap and a chat with the bartender. Wasn't it Richie on shift tonight? He'd always liked her. Perhaps he could make her feel better, for a while.

* * * * * * * * *

Buddy couldn't sleep. Beside him, Cindy-Lou dozed comfortably, her angelic face free from worry. That was just how Buddy liked it. He didn't want Cindy-Lou to ever have to worry about a thing. Certainly not about this business with 'Jimmy the Shark'. The man had been unhinged, but Buddy still felt bad about laying him out, and worse still, leaving him lying in the road. What if the cops got wind of it? They could be banging the hotel room door down any moment, and how would that look with his employer? The Air Force needed reliable men down on the base. Men who could keep a cool head. Who didn't lose their tempers and then run from the scene of the crime.

The sequence replayed in Buddy's mind, running round and round on a loop like a broken film reel. The car crashing. Jimmy's rambling. *It came from the sky. I saw it ... Round. Silver.*

They're coming. I can't see 'em, but they're coming.

Round. Silver. When Buddy closed his eyes, he could almost see it. *It came from the sky.*

He sat bolt upright, his veins filling with ice.

Jimmy wasn't drunk. He was afraid. So afraid he'd almost lost his senses. And Buddy had a horrible feeling he knew why.

★·☆·★·☆·★·☆·★·☆·★

Glitter threw on a pair of shorts and a t-shirt and headed downstairs. When she reached the lobby, she was surprised to see Buddy coming out of the elevator opposite. Their eyes met across the lurid carpet.

"Trouble sleeping?" Buddy asked when he got within earshot.

"Guess so," Glitter replied. "Want to get a drink?"

"What I need is a breath of fresh air. I was thinking about what Jimmy said." He glanced at her. "You're gonna think I'm crazy."

"Try me." Glitter followed him outside.

"I think there might be something in it … in this tumbleweed stuff, I mean. Jimmy talked about seeing something fall from the sky and, well—"

Buddy stopped. Glitter didn't have to ask what had distracted him. Tumbleweeds were blowing all over the parking lot, skittering across empty parking spaces, piling up against cars. Down the road, she could see even more of them drifting along—a whole tidal wave of them, like an advancing army. She stared at them for a long moment, trying to work out what it was about them that made her uneasy. Tumbleweed deluges did happen, now and then, when there was a bumper crop of the plants and the wind blew in the right direction.

Only—that was it.

The wind *wasn't* blowing in the right direction. In fact, it was hardly blowing at all. Yet the tumbleweeds drifted all the same, rolling along the strip, causing the few cars that were still moving to skid to a halt.

"I need to speak to Jimmy," Buddy said. She could tell from his thoughtful expression that he'd noticed the uncanny lack of wind, too. "Do you know where I can find him?"

Glitter shook her head. "I don't think that's a good idea."

"But you do know?"

She hesitated. "He'll be real mad …"

"This is important," Buddy insisted. "This is … Well, if my suspicions are right, it could be a matter of national security."

Something in his tone persuaded Glitter that he was deadly serious. She looked again at the road, the eerie way the tumbleweeds bounced along, their movements strangely purposeful.

She shuddered.

"All right," she said, still reluctant. "Jimmy owns a bar on Fremont Street. That's the best place to look."

⁕⁕⁕⁕⁕⁕⁕⁕

Buddy drove while Glitter gave directions to Fremont Street. It was a slow journey, because the mass of tumbleweeds blocked most of the roads. In the end, they parked a block down from Jimmy's bar, beneath the grinning figure of Vegas Vic in his Stetson, and walked the rest of the way.

Even so late at night, Fremont Street was still lit up like a slot machine. Cars parked bumper-to-bumper outside the hotels and casinos, and every sign blinked with dazzling lights, trying to entice the folks stumbling down the sidewalk. The well-heeled tourist-types were long gone, and those remaining were the mobsters and their molls, the down-and-out gamblers, the showgirls-turned-hookers who stood on the street corners, their world-weary snarls a warning to Glitter about what happened when a dancing girl's looks faded.

A drunk stumbled out of a dark side-street, swearing. His trousers were ripped to shreds, revealing bleeding skin beneath.

"That stuff!" he yelled, pointing a shaking finger at a pile of tumbleweeds resting against the doorway of a strip joint.

"That stuff is lethal. Look!" He tried to accost Glitter as she passed him by. "Look what it did to me!"

"Come on." Buddy put a hand on the small of Glitter's back, leading her away as though he was her boyfriend—or client, more like, at this end of town. "We've got to get to Jimmy's. I need to know what we're dealing with here, so I can call my—"

"Hey! Hey, that's him! That's the guy!"

Distracted by the drunk, Glitter hadn't realized they were close to Jimmy's Bar until they were almost on top of it. The single-story building nestled incongruously amongst the taller structures, and her plans to sidle in unnoticed were ruined by the fact that Jimmy himself stood outside the door, smoking and chatting with his cronies. His nose looked severely out of joint, and one of his eyes was starting to bruise, but other than that he seemed back to his usual self, which didn't bode well for Glitter—or Buddy.

"Come back for some more?" he asked, squaring up to Buddy. He folded his arms and stood with his legs apart, jutting his chin, cigarette still smoldering between his fingers. His face was half-hidden by his fedora.

"I only wanted to talk to you." Buddy held his palms out.

"Oh-ho-ho. The kid wants to talk." Jimmy laughed, looking round at his friends for support. They sniggered on cue. Satisfied, he turned back to Buddy. "You got something on your mind, big shot?"

"About what you saw," Buddy went on. "Out in the desert. You told me something fell from the sky."

Glitter knew they'd made a serious error of judgement. Jimmy was standing here, outside, as the tumbleweeds he'd been so afraid of filled the street, and he wasn't flinching. He wasn't going to admit to being frightened of anything now—not in front of his associates.

"I don't know what you're talkin' about." He looked Buddy up and down with narrowed eyes. "I didn't see nothin' out there."

"Then you're not worried about these?" Buddy indicated the tumbleweeds.

"Bunch of damn tumbleweeds? Why the heck would I be worried about that?" Jimmy sneered and took a drag of his cigarette, but Glitter noticed him dart a glance at the tumbleweeds. He seemed tense. Jittery, although he was doing his best to hide it.

"Buddy," she whispered, "let's go."

"This is important," Buddy persisted. "It could be a matter of national security. Let me show you—"

He was reaching into his jacket before Glitter could stop him. The henchmens' reactions were more honed. They threw themselves on him like hounds, grabbing his arms and pinning them behind his back.

"My ID," Buddy said, placidly, making no attempt to struggle. "I only wanted to show you my ID."

Jimmy dropped his cigarette and stubbed it out with his shoe. Then, taking his time, he stepped up to Buddy and spat in his face.

"Bring him inside." He turned to walk into the bar, before glancing back over his shoulder at Glitter. "And the doll."

7

Cindy-Lou woke to an empty bed and a note on her nightstand. She snatched it from the pad and read it hurriedly. It was from Buddy, saying that he'd had trouble sleeping and had gone for an early morning walk. He told her not to worry, and that he would be back by breakfast time. Cindy-Lou glanced at the clock. It was almost nine. Surely he ought to have been back already?

She was used to Buddy being mysterious. It was his way, and his job demanded it. Still, she supposed some part of her had believed that once they were married, that would change. A husband didn't keep secrets from his wife. Not in Cindy-Lou's imagination. And yet here they were, only a few days after their wedding, and already he was lying to her.

Because it *was* a lie, she was sure. It had been clear the night before that the business with Jimmy the Shark had been playing on his mind. He'd lapsed into a distracted silence as they got ready for bed, and when Cindy-Lou had tried to give him a goodnight hug, he'd returned it perfunctorily, before turning straight over to go to sleep. Cindy-Lou had lain awake for a while, listening to him toss and turn, before she herself had drifted off.

And now she woke to find him gone, and she was worried. Very worried. Where could he possibly have gone on his own in Las Vegas? Was he looking for Jimmy? Or was there something else to his absence … perhaps something to do with that showgirl, Glitter? She was older, sure, but very pretty, and she'd been walking around in nothing but a jewel-encrusted bikini the whole time the two of them were together. Just what had passed between them, while Cindy-Lou had been left with Dean Valentine?

The thought of Dean made Cindy-Lou shudder. To think she'd let him get so close to her! She loved her husband, and he loved her—she was certain of that. No, there was no way he'd left her to spend time with some tacky chorus-girl. It would be much more like Buddy to have gone looking for Jimmy the Shark, to make sure that the mobster wasn't too badly hurt. Which, if Glitter's assessment of the man was to be believed, meant Buddy could be in danger. Right now.

Cindy-Lou sat up sharply. She swung her legs out of bed and dressed as quickly as she could, pulling on a sundress and tying her hair up in her signature ponytail. Grabbing her purse, she hurried out of the room, only to stop dead in the hallway when she realized she had no idea where she was going. She didn't know anyone in this town, and she didn't have a clue where to start looking for Jimmy. There was only one person she could think of to turn to, and for a moment she hesitated, unable to bear the thought. But Buddy might need her. She had no choice.

She was going to have to ask Dean Valentine for help.

She remembered him mentioning that he stayed in the penthouse suite, and so she took the elevator to the top floor. It opened to a small lobby with more of the same swirling carpet as downstairs, and only one door. Cindy-Lou hurried over and knocked.

No answer.

She knocked again. Still silence.

"Mr. Valentine?" she called in a timid voice. "Mr. Valentine, are you awake?"

She thought she heard a groan and a rustle of sheets from within, and, feeling emboldened, knocked again.

"Mr. Valentine, I'm so sorry to disturb you, but it's important!"

There was a long silence. Cindy-Lou raised her arm, prepared to knock one final time, when suddenly the door flew open.

"I hope you're not gonna slap me again," Dean drawled.

Cindy-Lou lowered her hand. Dean had opened the door

dressed only in a red velour robe, tied loosely so his dark chest hair was visible. A cigarette smoldered in his hand. Behind him, on the glass table in the middle of the sitting room, she noticed an empty whiskey bottle, a stack of his own records, and Glitter's feather headdress. Her eyes lingered on this last item for a moment before traveling back up to Dean's face.

"I'm looking for Buddy," she said. "Have you seen him?"

Dean took a drag of his cigarette and scrutinized her, letting the silence between them stretch out.

"Can't say that I have," he said at last. "Lost your old man, have you? What makes you think I'd know where he is?"

He was irritated with her, Cindy-Lou realized. Suddenly, she was very aware of how big he was. She thought of an article she'd read about him in the paper once, which had described him as a war veteran and ex-bare-knuckle boxer, who'd grown up amongst Italian immigrants in Brooklyn. She thought of the rumors her father had told her, about his having paid a mobster to get him his breakout role in *Mississippi Belles.* She thought about the fact that he was, by his own admission, a close personal friend of Jimmy the Shark. For the first time, all the puzzle pieces slotted together in Cindy-Lou's mind in a way they never had before, and she realized the man she was talking to was no romantic hero like the ones he played in the movies. Suddenly she felt very small and very vulnerable.

"I—I'm sorry to have disturbed you," she said. "And I'm sorry for—for slapping you last night. You startled me, that's all. I didn't mean anything by it."

"Sure you didn't, Popsicle." Dean bared his white teeth in a smile that could've graced the cover of one of his LPs, but that nonetheless felt false.

"I'll just go and look for my husband. Maybe the concierge ..."

"Now, now, don't be hasty. Why don't you come in a minute and tell me what's going on?"

Dean stepped aside to give her room to pass, his eyes never leaving her face.

Cindy-Lou hesitated, then headed inside. She took a seat on one end of the white leather sofa, folding her hands in her lap.

"I'm worried about Buddy." She watched Dean pour two glasses of orange juice from the minibar. "He went out some time in the night and left me a note saying he'd be back for breakfast, only there's no sign of him. I'm afraid ..." her voice quivered. "I'm afraid he's gone looking for Jimmy the Shark."

Dean handed her a glass of juice and sat down beside

her, a little too close. "Well, you're welcome to have breakfast here. I'll order room service."

"Mr. Valentine!" Tears sprung to Cindy-Lou's eyes. "This is serious!"

"If your old man is stupid enough to go seeking out Jimmy without waiting for me to have a word, let him. The boy thinks he's some kind of hero." He settled back against the cushions. "He'll soon realize there are no heroes in Vegas. Only wise guys and dead ones. Do you get my drift?"

"Well, if you won't help me, I'll have to find him myself." Cindy-Lou got to her feet.

Dean tutted. "Sit down, enjoy some breakfast. I'm sure he'll be back safe and sound before the breakfast buffet closes."

"I can't just sit here and wait, Mr. Valentine!"

"Well, you sure as hell can't go looking for Jimmy on your own."

"I don't believe I have any choice."

Dean sighed. "You're a stubborn one. At least wait for me to get dressed."

"Then you'll come with me?"

Dean hoisted himself to his feet. "I can't let you go wandering down to Fremont Street all by yourself. You'll be eaten alive. Give me five minutes, then we'll go and see what Jimmy has to say for himself."

"Oh, thank you, Mr. Valentine! Thank you!"

"Hold your horses, Popsicle. There's a chance your old man's gotten himself mixed up in something he doesn't understand, and I'm not making any guarantees that I can get him out of it."

"Of course," Cindy-Lou said. "I understand." As Dean went through to the bedroom, she pressed her fingers to her lips. "Gosh darn it, Buddy. Why'd you have to go and do something so stupid?"

****

Cindy-Lou followed Dean through the early morning quiet of the hotel lobby, hurrying to keep up with him. He opened the door, held it for her, and she stepped out into chaos.

Tumbleweeds were piled high in the parking lot and along much of the road beyond. A landslide of plants had descended overnight, bringing the city to a complete standstill. All along the strip, drivers leaned out of car windows, shouting and honking their horns. Several had abandoned their cars and sat or stood at the side of the road, looking bemused and frustrated.

"What the heck are these things doing on my baby?" Dean stormed over to the sea-green Cadillac parked by the door and swept his arm across the bonnet, dislodging the weeds that had gathered there.

"Goddamnit—Ow! Jesus Christ!"

"What is it?" As the weeds skittered away, Cindy-Lou hurried over. Dean turned to her, clutching his wrist.

"That stuff scratched me."

Cindy-Lou peered at his arm. Sure enough, a ragged red slash sliced through his skin. She winced.

"That's more than a scratch. It looks deep."

Dean flexed his fingers. "It's nothing."

Cindy-Lou crept over to one of the weeds and peered at it. In the bright sunlight, the dry tangle of branches looked almost silvery.

"It must have thorns." She reached out to touch it, then pulled back, flinching. A red bead of blood formed on her finger. "Ouch! It's sharp, like … like razor wire."

"Careful." Dean scanned the horizon. "If these things are dangerous, we'd be better off heading back inside. Hunker down until somebody clears this crap away and we can drive again."

"No." Cindy-Lou shook her head. "No, I can't just hide away. Buddy might be in trouble."

"You want to get to Fremont Street, you're gonna have to walk." Dean patted the Cadillac's bonnet. "I'm not taking my baby out in this."

"Then I'll walk, Mr. Valentine. Just tell me the way."

Dean stared at her for a long moment. "You could get yourself hurt, you know that? Or worse."

Cindy-Lou jutted her chin and didn't move. Eventually, Dean sighed.

"Fine," he said. "We'll walk."

The sun beat down as they traveled up the strip, carefully picking their way around the tumbleweeds. The air was as dry as a tinderbox, and Cindy-Lou soon wished she had some water. Worse than the heat, though, was the chaos surrounding them. Dean wasn't the only person injured by the tumbleweeds—all along the road victims sat in tattered clothes, nursing gouged ankles and scratched arms.

A janitor emerged from a nearby hotel with a broom to brush the weeds away, and Cindy-Lou watched in horror as the plants swarmed over him, knocking him to the ground in their haste to get through the open door. He vanished, screaming, beneath the tangle. Cindy-Lou tried to run to him, but Dean grabbed her arm, pulling her back.

"Don't get close to them."

"We ought to help him!"

"You can't help him—just look."

The weeds vanished inside the hotel, leaving the janitor

curled up on the ground in a fetal position. Dean let go of Cindy-Lou, and she crept towards the man. His arms were clutched around his knees, and he wasn't moving. The tumbleweeds had shredded the skin of his face and arms into thin ribbons, his flesh hanging off exposed bone. Blood oozed from beneath his torn clothes, staining his blue shirt and trousers a dark brownish red. His eyes were wide open, staring—well, one of them was. The other hung dislodged from its socket, resting on his cheek with only a thin strand of nerve keeping it attached.

Cindy-Lou took a step back. Then another. She wanted to stop looking—*needed* to stop looking—but she couldn't turn away. Couldn't even blink.

The last time she'd seen that much blood was … was …

No, she couldn't think of that.

Her head span. Black spots invaded her vision, and she was glad of them, because they chased away the sight of the janitor. But when she closed her eyes he returned, his corpse emblazoned on her eyelids, and she remembered the blood. All that blood. A familiar pain twisted deep in her stomach.

She screamed.

When Cindy-Lou came to, she was sitting propped up

against the wall, in an unfamiliar hotel lobby. Dean crouched near her, holding a paper cup.

"Here," he said, handing it to her. "Have some water. You'll feel better soon."

"What happened?"

"You fainted. Don't blame you. That wasn't a sight anyone oughta see."

Cindy-Lou sipped at her water. "He—he was—"

"Try not to think about it."

"Those plants ... they're terrifying!"

"Tell me about it." Dean sat beside her.

"They went into the hotel like ... like they meant to. Like they were looking for something." Cindy-Lou looked around in panic, half-expecting to see tumbleweeds creeping out from every corner.

"Don't worry," Dean said. "There's none in here. I checked. We'll stay here, wait this out. Get a message to the Peacock so that your old man'll know where we are if he gets back there."

Cindy-Lou shook her head. "No. No, I can't just stay here. Not without knowing Buddy's okay. What if one of those things got him?"

Dean sighed. "You're tougher than you look, ain't you?"

"Inside I'm shaking," Cindy-Lou replied, "but that's not going to make me give up on my husband."

Dean glanced at her with grudging admiration. "He's a lucky guy." He sighed. "I just hope Glitz stayed safe at the Peacock. I don't like to think of her out there somewhere, in the middle of all this."

Cindy-Lou patted his arm. "We'll find her, too," she said. "She'll be okay."

Once Cindy-Lou had recovered enough to leave the hotel, she and Dean headed back out onto the strip. They agreed that their best course of action was to keep a low profile and avoid bothering the tumbleweeds—the plants only seemed to attack those who got in their way. Otherwise, they just sort of … *sat there*, rustling, piled up in the middle of the street. Cindy-Lou watched them out of the corner of her eye as they walked by, wondering why they were there. What were they doing? Did they think, or did they just react on instinct, like frightened animals?

On the next corner, they came upon a pair of police officers, huddled behind their car in a stand-off with a wall of tumbleweeds on the other side of the road.

"Hey," one of them called, "you folks shouldn't be out here. It's not safe!"

He turned and fired a few shots into the tumbleweed wall, which wobbled, but showed no other reaction.

"Officer Kepler?" Dean shouted from a safe distance. "What the heck is going on?"

"We don't know," Kepler called back. "But the place is crawling with these things, and they ain't no ordinary plants. People have died. Go back to your hotel. Get inside. Anywhere. You can't stay out here."

Dean looked at Cindy-Lou, who regarded him levelly.

"How much farther to Fremont Street?" she asked.

Dean paused, gazing down the street. "A couple more blocks."

More gunfire. Somebody screamed. Cindy-Lou clutched at Dean's arm again. All she wanted was to get somewhere safe. But she couldn't. Not yet. Not without Buddy.

"We can make it," she said. "If we're quick. Come on."

8

The storeroom of Jimmy's bar smelled of beer and mildew. Glitter and Buddy sat back-to-back on hard wooden chairs, their wrists tied behind them. The rope bit into Glitter's skin every time she moved. Jimmy and his cronies had secured them here hours ago and then disappeared—Glitter had no idea where.

For a while, Buddy tried shouting for them to come back, before finally lapsing into a defeated silence. Glitter watched the tiny window near the ceiling as the darkness outside was slowly replaced by a pale, sickly light.

As the Nevada sun slunk sidelong through the window, Buddy let out something between a groan and a sob.

"Cindy-Lou'll be awake by now," he said. "What's she going to think when she finds out I'm not there?"

"She's fine. She's safe. Don't you worry about her. Worry about *us*." Glitter couldn't keep a tinge of bitterness out of her voice. It was Buddy's fault they were here in the first place. If he'd only *listened* to her.

"What happens when Jimmy gets back?"

Glitter sighed. "Depends what kinda mood he's in. Maybe, if we're lucky, he'll think we've had enough of a scare and just let us go."

"And if we're not lucky …?"

"That ain't worth thinking about, believe me."

"You know what scares me most?" Buddy said.

"Sure I'm gonna hear about it either way."

"I'm afraid Cindy-Lou will work out where I've gone and come looking for me. I left her a note saying I'd be back by breakfast. When that doesn't happen, she'll worry. She might put two-and-two together. She's an intelligent girl," he added, with a note of pride. "But I don't want her out on the streets right now. If only I could get a message to her somehow. Tell her to stay in the hotel."

"Well, you can't," Glitter snapped. "So how's about you use that big brain of yours and help me figure out a way to get out of here?"

Buddy was silent. Glitter strained at her ropes again, but the more she struggled the deeper they cut.

"Perhaps if I could just *talk* to Jimmy," Buddy mused. "If he'd only give me a fair hearing, I'm sure he'd see sense."

"Jimmy ain't gonna give you a fair hearing, and he wouldn't know what sense was if it came up and slapped him in the face. Whatever happened to him last night's got him rattled, and that'll make him more unpredictable than ever." She paused. "Those things out there … the tumbleweeds … what are they really, Bud? You know something, I can tell."

"I don't know much," Buddy replied. "But from what I've seen so far, and the way Jimmy described the object falling from the sky … well, I don't think he's wrong to be rattled." He paused. "This goes no further, you understand me?"

"Sure."

"All right. Back at the base a couple weeks ago, a ranger called us about something he'd found in the desert. A couple of guys went down to check it out. It was a crash site—a crater. At first they thought the thing inside was a meteorite, but when they got close, they realized it was no natural formation. It was silver, disc-shaped, similar to what Jimmy described. They suspected man-made. Russians, perhaps.

"So they took this thing back to base and got me to start running tests on it, in one of the empty aircraft hangars. The substance it's made from—it's not like anything on Earth. It looks like a metal, but it has … memory, I guess. It can take on the properties of whatever it comes into contact with."

"What does that mean? What's it got to do with the

tumbleweeds?"

Buddy hesitated. His chair creaked as he shifted position.

"I can't be sure," he said. "It's just a theory. But I'm afraid those things out there aren't tumbleweeds at all. I don't think they're plants. I don't even think they're from this planet."

"You think they came from outer space?" The idea seemed so crazy that Glitter couldn't help but laugh, but when he spoke again, Buddy's voice was deadly serious.

"Yeah," he said. "Yeah, I do. I'd wager what Jimmy saw crash-land was another of those discs, like the one I've been researching. And if something came out of this one, something made from this shape-shifting substance … Well, the tumbleweed form is probably just the first thing it came across on Earth. And that means by now it could be anything. Do anything."

"You think it can … change shape?"

"It's possible."

Glitter thought of the tumbleweeds lining the streets. Could Buddy be right? Could it be … *planning something*? And suddenly, out of nowhere, she thought of Dean, lounging totally unaware in his suite. Probably puffing away on a cigar as some kind of alien invader lined the streets. Not to mention all the other people out there.

"We're the only ones who know about this?" she said in a quiet voice.

"At the moment, yes. We most likely are. If only I could get to a telephone, I could call the base. Alert them of the threat. But right now …"

"We've got to get out of here." Glitter swept the room with her eyes, hunting for something, *anything*, that might help them escape before Jimmy returned. There was nothing useful amongst the beer kegs and boxes that surrounded them. The only exit, other than the locked door, was the tiny window she'd been staring at all night. If they could prize it open, they might just about be able to wriggle through. But first they had to get to it.

She rolled one shoulder back, then the other, repeating the motion again and again whilst straightening her arms as much as she could. The chair rocked with each movement.

"What are you doing?" Buddy complained. "You're going to tip us over."

"I did a routine years ago," Glitter said, grimacing as the ropes dug into her skin. "Dean had a song called *All Tied Up*. I had to get out … from a knot like this … by bending my elbows back the wrong way and wriggling it … looser until I could get my thumb under the ropes, and … got it!"

Buddy craned his neck, trying to look at her as the rope tumbled to the floor. "How did you do that?"

Glitter shook her arms out to get the blood flowing through them again. "I'm double jointed. Guess it gives me a bit of extra wiggle room." She turned to untie Buddy. As his rope came loose in her hands and he got to his feet, she pointed at the window. "Do you reckon you can reach that and get it open?"

"Sure thing." Buddy got hold of a nearby crate and dragged it over to the window, but as he prepared to climb onto it, Glitter heard footsteps approaching, and held up a hand. Buddy grabbed a beer bottle from out of the crate and stood behind the door.

"Sit back down," he hissed, "and get ready to run."

Glitter did as she was told, perching back on her seat just as the door flew open.

The moment Jimmy stepped through the door, Buddy smacked him hard on the head with the beer bottle. Jimmy staggered back, and Glitter and Buddy darted past him into the bar itself, only to find their way blocked by several of Jimmy's shady-looking henchmen. Within seconds, they had their arms pinned behind their backs yet again, and as they struggled, Jimmy re-emerged from the back, rubbing his head. Glitter stared, amazed to see him so unscathed.

"You," he snarled at Buddy. "You must have a death wish. Sit them down," he added, ignoring Buddy's protests. Glitter found herself shoved into a nearby booth, Buddy beside her. Jimmy loomed over them, eyes darting from one face to the other.

"What do you know?" he asked, his voice uncharacteristically level.

"Know?" Buddy ventured.

"You know something about the tumbleweeds. You were asking questions. What do you know?"

Glitter and Buddy exchanged a look. There was something eerie about the calmness with which Jimmy spoke. It didn't feel like him.

Buddy raised his hands in a placating gesture. "Mr. … ah …?"

"Catalano."

"Mr. Catalano. Please listen to me. I need to access a telephone urgently."

"Not until you answer my question."

He clicked his fingers and one of Jimmy's cronies stepped forward, a knife in his hand.

"There ain't no need for that," Glitter said quickly. "Buddy'll explain what he knows, won't you, Bud?"

Buddy took a deep breath. "Mr. Catalano, I work for the US government, over at the air force base past Indian Springs."

"So it *does* exist," piped up a henchman. Jimmy silenced him with a glare.

Buddy went on: "Lately, we've been investigating an un-identified object that crashed in the desert. A craft of some kind that we believe came from outer space. I think what you saw last night might have been related to it. Put simply, those tumbleweeds out there aren't tumbleweeds at all. I be-lieve they're of extra-terrestrial origin."

Jimmy paced up and down in front of them, his hands behind his back. "Go on."

"Mr. Catalano, this is a matter of national security, and I need to speak to my superiors immediately." Buddy held up his hands. "I won't say a word about you, or anything that's happened here. I just need to warn them so they can send help."

Jimmy stared at Buddy, his face blank. For a moment, Glitter thought he would relent, but when he spoke again there was a chill in his voice.

"I can't let you do that." His eyes flashed strangely, his irises taking on a silvery sheen. Glitter felt as uneasy as a gambler on a losing streak.

"But Mr. Catalano …" Buddy began.

"Secure them. Do it properly this time."

Jimmy removed his fedora, placing it on the bar. He ran a hand through his thinning hair, and Glitter was sure his skin glowed. Then her view was blocked by one of his henchmen, who grabbed her arm and pulled her to her feet to force her back into the storeroom.

9

By the time Cindy-Lou and Dean reached Fremont Street, the sidewalks were crowded with people. Some had been forced to stop their cars by the tumbleweeds that flowed down the street like a tangled, razor-sharp river. Others had emerged from their hotels and gambling dens to gawp at the invasion. People ran in all directions, into and out of buildings, to and from their abandoned vehicles—there was no purpose or reason to any of it. Tourists gathered in groups, snapping photographs and chattering amongst themselves as though the whole thing was just another show.

As Cindy-Lou and Dean jostled through the crowd, the tumbleweeds descended on one particularly fearless photographer who'd rushed into the road to get a shot of the wave. Finding he couldn't get out of the way fast enough, he staggered and tripped, sprawling on his back with his mouth open in horror as the weeds engulfed him.

Cindy-Lou turned away, hiding her face in Dean's arm. Her legs were shaking so hard she could barely stand. From what she could tell, the tumbleweeds were attempting to enter each building in turn and anyone who stood in their way, even unintentionally, got torn to shreds. Survivors stumbled out of casinos with flayed skin hanging from their bones, wailing like the zombies Cindy-Lou had once seen in a late-night B-movie. Some fell in the road ahead of where she and Dean walked, and all she could do was mutter a little prayer as she passed them by and thank God they didn't have to suffer anymore.

But surely it was only a matter of time until she and Dean shared the same fate? Why hadn't she taken his advice and stayed in the hotel? As people retreated indoors, barricading themselves in as best they could with whatever furniture they had to hand, Cindy-Lou was tempted to join them. Only her determination to find Buddy kept her going.

Dean walked in silence, his jaw set like marble, seemingly oblivious to Cindy-Lou clinging to his arm. As they reached the corner of the block, he stopped, scanning the street ahead. The further they walked, the worse things seemed to get. It was like a war zone. Bodies lay everywhere, alongside the smoldering remains of wrecked cars. Tumbleweeds were piled high along the sidewalks, rustling threateningly.

Dean pulled Cindy-Lou behind an abandoned pickup truck, and together they peered out at the wreckage.

"This is madness," he muttered. "I haven't seen anything like this since the war."

"What did you do?" she asked. "In the war, I mean?"

"I fought in Manila."

"Was it like ..." Cindy-Lou cast her gaze around the street, at the bodies, the blood, only half-seeing. "Was it like this?"

"More Japs, less weeds," Dean replied. "Otherwise, not that different. See that green sign? Just down from the Lucky Strike Club? That's Jimmy's Bar. If Buddy really went looking for him, he'll be there."

"How are we going to get past the tumbleweeds?"

"It's not far," Dean said. "We need to run. Are you ready?"

"Yes," Cindy-Lou whispered, taking a small step back.

"All right. Run!"

He grabbed her hand and they fled down the sidewalk. Cindy-Lou looked over her shoulder to see dozens—even hundreds—of tumbleweeds bouncing after them like balls poured from a bucket. She screamed, and at the same moment Dean yanked her round a corner, and they flew down a back alley into a yard full of empty beer kegs. They ran for the door and pounded on it, yelling as loud as they could. When the first few tumbleweeds entered the yard, Cindy-Lou was sure they were done for. She turned, her back pressed against the door, and screamed again as the balls bounded towards her.

Then the door flew open, and she stumbled back. Somebody caught her around the waist.

"Stop," he said.

The tumbleweeds stopped. The plants that had been about to rip Dean and Cindy-Lou apart fell to the ground like stones and lay there, dead still.

Cindy-Lou looked up at her savior. He wore a pinstripe suit and a fedora, and a scar ran down his left cheek. But she only had an instant to take these things in before she noticed his eyes. His *eyes*. The irises shone silver, and they seemed to *move*, flowing like molten mercury. She gasped and tried to take a step back, but the man kept his grip on her waist. He stood unmoving, as though he was waiting for something.

"Jimmy?" Dean said.

The gangster turned his head slowly in Dean's direction and stared at him. The silver glow blazing from Jimmy's eyes was so bright that Dean had to squint.

"Jimmy?" he repeated. "What the heck's the matter with you?"

Jimmy dropped his arm from around Cindy-Lou's waist.

"Come inside," he said, before turning and walking back into the bar.

Cindy-Lou looked at Dean, who shrugged.

"Ladies first."

10

"Hey, what the hell is this?"

Glitter's heart beat faster at the sound of the familiar voice. She and Buddy were tied up in their seats once more, but this time Jimmy had left a guard in the room. She'd all but given up on the idea of getting free when she heard the scuffle just outside.

"Hey Jimmy, what's going on? Don't you recognize me? Tell these bozos who I am!"

The door flew open. Dean stumbled in backwards, tripped and fell on his ass. Glitter almost laughed at the sheer indignation on his face. Then she realized how relieved she was to see him and laughed for real.

Cindy-Lou followed him in, dragged through by one of Jimmy's henchmen. Her eyes brightened when she saw Buddy.

"Bud! Thank goodness you're alive!" She turned to Jimmy, whose broad-shouldered figure now blocked the doorway. "Say, couldn't you untie him? He won't do anything, I swear."

Jimmy nodded to his henchmen, and they pulled up two more chairs at right-angles to Glitter and Buddy's. Cindy-Lou sat in one of them, docile, and allowed herself to be secured. Dean, on the other hand, had to be dragged over, shouting and furious.

"You're signing your own death warrant, James Catalano!" he yelled. "You just—*oof.*"

Jimmy socked Dean hard in the face and shoved him into the seat alongside Glitter, where he sat pinching his nose, blood spewing over his white shirt.

"Jesus Christ," Dean spluttered. "Jesus Goddamn Christ. Haven't you seen what's going on out there?"

Jimmy pulled Dean's hands away from his face and secured them, then stepped back, staring down at the four of them.

"The invasion has begun," he said in a blank, metallic voice.

Glitter shivered.

"What do you mean?" she asked. "The invasion?"

But Jimmy was already heading out of the room. The door slammed behind him, leaving them alone with only their guard for company.

"The invasion?" Cindy-Lou said, in a small voice. Then she started to cry, sniffling loudly right next to Glitter's ear.

"It's gonna be fine, Cindy," Buddy murmured. "It's all gonna be fine."

"Bud …" Cindy-Lou whimpered. "You didn't see what I saw. Out on the streets. It's awful. People are dead! And that—that Jimmy … he stopped them. The tumbleweeds were about to kill us, and he stopped them with one word. How did he do that?"

For a moment, nobody spoke. Glitter stared at the window. She could feel the others thinking, even though she couldn't see them. *How* did *he do that?* Jimmy had been the first to encounter the tumbleweeds. The only one to survive, if his story was to be believed. And ever since he'd returned to Las Vegas he'd been acting strange.

"Buddy …" she began. "D'you think that's … not really Jimmy?"

"It's not possible," Buddy said, shortly.

"Why not? You said it could change shape. Be anything. Do anything."

"But a human organism? No, that's too complex. In the lab, we found the alien substance could emulate simple, inanimate objects. Tumbleweeds, yes, that's a real possibility. A human being? No, I don't think so."

"Did you ever try it?" Glitter replied. "Well? Did you?"

"No, but …"

"So you don't know."

"I ..."

"You don't *know*," Glitter repeated. "It coulda 'emulated' Jimmy when it found him there in the desert, couldn't it?"

"I don't think it's as simple as—"

"It coulda, couldn't it?"

"What are you talking about?" Cindy-Lou wailed.

"Yeah," Dean cut in. "Want to catch the rest of us up?"

Buddy repeated what he'd told Glitter about his work at the air base. When he finished, the other three were silent for some time. Eventually, Dean spoke.

"So, what you're saying is, Jimmy might not be Jimmy? He's really an ... *alien* ... pretending to be Jimmy?"

"That's right," said Glitter.

"Not exactly," Buddy said, at the same time.

"Not exactly?" Glitter frowned up at the window. It must've been getting on for noon, judging by the shaft of sunlight shining directly down on her.

"When we saw Jimmy last night, he seemed like himself, right?" Buddy said.

Glitter made a face. "Well, I wouldn't say exactly that ..."

"All right, he was shook up, but he seemed ... normal. Human. We didn't notice anything out of the ordinary about him until this morning."

"I guess not."

"So perhaps the substance didn't replace him completely, back there in the desert," Buddy went on. "Like I said, an entire human being is too complex for it to emulate. It can copy simple structures, but for a human being, perhaps it takes a different strategy. Not making a full copy of the entire person, but entering their bloodstream, replicating simple cells over and over until it gains control over their speech, thoughts, movement …"

"All right, Einstein," Dean snapped. "Why don't you explain what you're talking about in words the rest of us can understand?"

"Sure," said Buddy. "What I'm trying to say is, this extra-terrestrial substance might have caught Jimmy, but it let him go again. It entered his bloodstream, then allowed him to continue unawares back to Vegas. Since then, it's been multiplying inside him, learning how he functions, perhaps also learning about the rest of us, and the world around it, as well. All this has made his behavior even more erratic and unpredictable than usual, until now, finally, the alien's asserting control. There's still some of Jimmy left in there, but there may not be for much longer."

"Can't say that made a bit of goddamn sense to me," Dean replied.

"Well, it makes sense to me," Glitter said, still watching

the window. "Enough that I know we've been captured by some kinda alien ... thing. I sure don't want to hang about here and find out what he's planning." She grimaced. "Maybe if there's still a bit of Jimmy in there, we could talk to him again, persuade him ..."

"I think it's probably too late for that," Buddy cut in.

"But what does he want with us?" said Cindy-Lou.

"It's possible he doesn't even know himself," said Buddy. "I don't know what's controlling these shapeshifters. From my research, I had the impression they were pretty simple, single-celled structures. They can band together, follow basic instructions, but I doubt they have the capability to think. Something else must be controlling them. Issuing them orders. Like ..."

"Like a military general," Dean finished.

Buddy's silence betrayed his surprise.

"Yes," he said, after a moment. "Yes, that's exactly it."

"Jimmy's a military man," said Dean. "That's how I know him. I was his commanding officer."

"Sure, but—"

"So maybe I can find a way to get through to him."

"Well, I don't think—"

"Hey!" Dean yelled at the top of his voice, making Glitter flinch. "Hey you! Bozo. Yeah, I'm talking to you."

From where she sat, Glitter couldn't see the guard

approaching, but she could hear his footsteps on the concrete floor. His shadow loomed over them as he stood in front of Dean.

"Quit your noise or I'll have to get the boss back in."

"Yeah, do that," Dean shouted. "Go ahead, go get Jimmy. Tell him I want to give him a piece of my mind. Go on! Jimmy! JIMMY! Come on back in here, you coward!"

The henchman left the room, and there was the sound of discussion in the corridor before Jimmy himself returned, alone.

"Is there a problem?" Jimmy's voice rang through the room.

"Yeah, there's a goddamn problem," Dean yelled. "You're out of line, Private. D'you hear me? If you don't untie me *right now,* you're risking a court martial, understood? Do you know what we do to traitors? *Do you*?"

Silence. Glitter held her breath. Jimmy's face, as much as she could see of it beneath his fedora, looked completely blank.

"You want me … to untie you?" There was a note of doubt in Jimmy's voice. Not much, but enough to give Glitter some hope.

"I gave you an order, soldier," Dean replied.

Jimmy's eyes glinted. He frowned at Dean, his expression crumbling.

"S-sergeant Valentino?"

"Did you hear my order, Private? Untie me."

Jimmy's eyes flickered from silver to brown and back again as he surveyed the room. "Where am I? What's happening?"

Realizing he was distracted, Glitter started working on her own ropes, hoping to repeat the escape trick she'd used before.

"Japs got us, Catalano," Dean said. "Tied me up. We need to get outta here, quick."

"That can't—No. It's not happening. That's—that's over." Jimmy reached up, gripping his head. "There's this noise. Buzzing. I can't get rid of it. I can't shut it up!"

"Untie me," Dean said.

Jimmy stared at him as though he was the only still point in a spinning room. His face was bleached white. Eventually, with shaking hands, he leaned down and started to untie Dean.

Dean didn't waste any time. The moment his hands were free, he jumped to his feet and punched Jimmy straight in the face. Jimmy rounded on him, but the blow had disoriented him, and Dean, the heavier of the two, got hold of him by the lapels. He slammed Jimmy against the wall and wedged his arm against Jimmy's windpipe. Jimmy's eyes bulged as he gasped for breath, flashing silver. He groped for Dean's throat, but had to settle for clinging to his jacket as he crumpled to the ground.

Glitter slipped her ropes just as the guard returned to see what the commotion was about. His eyes swept the room, taking in Jimmy's unconscious form and Dean, standing with his fists balled, staring him down. The guard opened his mouth to shout for backup, but before he could utter a word, Glitter leaped from her chair and hurled herself at him. She slammed her head into the guard's bulging stomach and staggered back, dizzy, suspecting that she'd hurt herself more than she had him. But it was enough to wind him, and he doubled over. Dean grabbed one of the discarded lengths of rope and advanced on the guard. He looped the rope around the man's thick neck, pulling it tight and yanking him onto his feet.

"Keep your mouth shut or you'll end up like him," he said, nodding toward Jimmy.

Glitter hurried to untie Buddy, then Cindy-Lou, while Buddy helped Dean restrain the guard. Together they pushed him back against the wall until he was forced to sit, then, using the makeshift noose, they lashed him to Jimmy so that neither of them could move without the other. Buddy tied their hands with the remaining rope.

Cindy-Lou headed for the door, but Glitter stopped her.

"That's a bad idea," she hissed. "There'll be more of 'em

coming any minute."

"So what now?"

Glitter pointed up. "The window. If we can squeeze outta there, we might be able to climb up onto the roof. Safe from Jimmy's guys, and safe from the tumbleweeds, too, I hope."

"Good idea." Buddy dragged a crate over beneath the window, and Glitter climbed up onto it, regretting that she'd worn heels. She pushed the window open and then, with Buddy's help to boost her up, wriggled through the tight gap. Her t-shirt snagged on the window frame, and she lost a shoe as she hoisted herself up onto the flat roof.

"Crap," she muttered, as she heard her stiletto hit the tarmac below. She scooted back from the edge until she felt safe, then pulled off the other shoe and tossed it aside. One shoe wouldn't be much use to her, anyway. Getting on her knees, she extended a hand to help Cindy-Lou clamber up beside her.

"Y'okay?" she asked, as Cindy-Lou dusted herself down. Somehow, the kid looked almost as pristine as ever in her poplin dress and petticoats. Only the tear tracks in her make-up betrayed the fact that she'd been crying.

"Yeah." She wiped her face with a handkerchief. "I'm fine."

Buddy was next to reach the roof, followed by Dean. As soon as he was up, Glitter got to her feet and pulled him into a hug.

"You got us out!"

"Guess I'm good for something, after all." Dean pulled away and held Glitter at arm's length, looking down at her.

"Did that bastard hurt you?"

Glitter shook her head. "I'm all in one piece. Unlike you." She indicated his broken nose, the blood on his face and collar. "We gotta get that seen to."

Dean prodded his nose gingerly. "It's been broken before. Perhaps it'll wind up straighter than it was."

Glitter allowed herself a faint smile, then turned to scan the horizon and the tumbleweeds lining the streets.

"Now what?" she asked.

"I need to get to a telephone," Buddy said. "Warn somebody about what's going on here. And then we need to get the heck out of Vegas."

11

"Where are we going to find a telephone?" Buddy paced the roof. "We can't stay here much longer."

It was midday, and the sun burned a hole in the clear blue sky. Cindy-Lou sat against the scaffolding that held up the sign for Jimmy's Bar. She was parched after her long walk, not to mention worried about the others. Dean's nose had stopped bleeding, but it looked painful, and Cindy-Lou could hardly bear to see the blood staining his white shirt. Buddy and Glitter both had raw skin around their wrists where the ropes had burned them. In the street below, tumbleweeds flowed over cars, each other, anyone still foolish enough to step into the road.

The gangsters hadn't come out looking for their captives. Perhaps they didn't dare, but surely it wouldn't be long until Jimmy the Shark woke, and he would be angry. Cindy-Lou felt like crying, but she bit back the tears. What good would they do?

"If we can get into the Lucky Strike, we can call

someone from there." Glitter pointed at a casino a short way down the block. "D'you think we can reach it?"

Buddy scanned the street.

"Maybe. It'd be safest to stay on the roofs, though, I reckon."

So they set out, clambering their way across rooftops and casino marquees. It was difficult, especially in the heat, but at least they were safe from the reach of the tumbleweeds. Eventually they reached the roof of the Lucky Strike. There they paused atop the bright red marquee, which screamed BINGO in tarnished gold letters down its length. Beside them, a pair of animatronic panhandlers sifted perpetually for gold, rictus grins on their faces.

Cindy-Lou peered over the edge of the marquee. Buddy's car was parked close by, half-buried in a drift of tumbleweeds.

"What do you think they want?" She looked down at the strange, tangled shapes. "Why are they doing this to us?"

"I'm not sure even they know," Buddy replied. "Sounds like the craft Jimmy saw must've crash-landed. My guess is they're acting on some kind of instinct. Maybe orders half-received, or remembered from a planned mission that went wrong when the first spaceship came down. I don't reckon they can think for themselves—not considering how Dean got through to the real Jimmy." He paused, looking thoughtful. "It's as though Jimmy's mind could override the alien's commands, even though Jimmy himself was unaware of what was really happening."

"Could be that Jimmy's the one who can't think for himself," Dean replied. "Some people are born to take orders."

Glitter looked around. "We need to get up to the main part of the roof. Should be a maintenance entrance up there, so's someone can get down here and fix the panhandlers if they break down. Come on."

She clambered onto the back of one of the panhandlers and hoisted herself onto the roof. Cindy-Lou and the others followed. The maintenance entrance was tucked away behind the rigging of the Lucky Strike's vast sign, and between them Dean and Buddy were able to break the flimsy lock and kick in the door. They hurried down the bare breeze-block staircase. As they approached the exit to the casino floor, the sound of a commotion came from the other side.

Carefully, Glitter edged the door open and peered out.

The casino had become a retreat for the injured. Holidaymakers and gamblers alike sat against the walls, nursing bleeding limbs. The hotel staff stood in a huddle close to the front doors, deep in discussion with a group of police officers who seemed to be refusing to let anybody leave. As Cindy-Lou and the others approached, an elderly couple dragging suitcases marched up to the officer in charge.

"Can't somebody tell us what's going on here?" demanded the husband. "We have a plane to catch."

"I'm sorry, sir." Sweat beaded on the officer's forehead. "We can't let anybody go out there right now."

"Well, why the heck not?" the husband persisted. "Are we supposed to miss our plane? Can't you at least give us an idea of what's happening?"

"Who's dealing with this?" His wife jabbed a finger at the cop. "All I see is you standing here, telling us we can't go outside. I want to talk to your superior."

"Ma'am, when you're able to leave, you'll be the first to know. For now, the situation is under control."

"Is it?" The wife leaned around him, trying to see out the glass doors. "It doesn't look that way to me."

She was right. Outside, the tumbleweeds had piled so high that it was almost impossible to see anything else. And they were moving, scratching, pressing against the glass. The doors creaked. The wife's eyes widened, and she backed away, grabbing her husband's arm. Seeing her expression, the cop turned, just as the doors crashed open and the tumbleweeds spewed into the casino. The wife let out an ear-piercing scream as the cop vanished beneath the plants. She batted the weeds with her handbag as they swamped her and her husband, swallowing them and their suitcases.

Buddy got in front of Cindy-Lou and the others, backing them up against a roulette table as the weeds spread out, pinballing across the casino floor. Slot machines tumbled, jangling and flashing, sending waves of silver coins splashing across the carpet. One gambler swept up an armful of nickels and tossed them at the tumbleweeds, only to be swiftly consumed.

"We gotta get out of here!" Glitter cried.

They raced back to the employee exit, joining a bottleneck of gamblers who'd had the same idea. Cindy-Lou tried to block out the screams behind her as the press of bodies shuffled through the door. Back in the corridor they were able to run again, carried by the tide of people out of the fire doors and into the road. Tumbleweeds rained down upon them from the roof like giant, vicious hailstones.

"The car!" Buddy shouted.

Cindy-Lou made a run for it, trying to shield her head with her arms, and was on the point of scrambling in when she heard Glitter shout.

"My ankle!"

Cindy-Lou turned. Glitter had fallen to her knees on the asphalt, holding her leg. Buddy grabbed her arm and pulled her to her feet, helping her into the back of the car just as Dean threw himself into the driver's seat.

Buddy jumped into the passenger side and tossed Dean

the keys.

"Drive, just drive!"

12

Dean slammed his foot onto the accelerator and the car sped off as tumbleweeds pummeled them from all directions, bouncing off the windscreen. Glitter huddled with Cindy-Lou in the back seat, nursing her injured ankle.

"Where are we going?" Glitter yelled.

"Yeah," Dean echoed. "Where *are* we going?"

"If we can get out of the city, we can drive to the base and find help," Buddy said. But as they turned onto the Strip, the car was already slowing. The tangle of tumble-weed was too dense. If they kept going much longer, it was bound to get wrapped around the wheels and burst a tire.

"We're not gonna get out of the city," Dean said. "We'll be lucky if we get as far as the Peacock."

"Then that's where we'll aim for." Buddy glanced back at the girls. "Glitter, are you all right? Will you be able to walk?"

"Do I have a choice?" The thought made Glitter wince, but the car was grinding to a halt, and they were still a couple blocks from the Peacock. Walking on her twisted ankle was the least of her worries when the street was swamped with tumbleweeds.

"Soon as we stop, get ready to run," Dean said. "It's clear enough down that side alley. If we can get around the block, we can go in the back way. Are you ready?"

"Ready," said Glitter.

"All right. Go!"

They flung themselves out of the car and fled down the alley, running as fast as they could. Pain shot up Glitter's leg with every step, stones and debris stabbing at her bare feet. Looking back, she saw the weeds behind them, bouncing around the corner, moving fast.

"Hurry, Glitter!" Cindy-Lou screamed.

The others were already far ahead, reaching the end of the block. Glitter couldn't keep up. The tumbleweeds were almost on top of her, and her goddamn leg refused to cooperate. It felt useless, like rubber.

Another step, and searing pain flamed through her. She stumbled. Fell, hands splayed out to catch herself on the concrete. Ignoring the jarring in her bones, she got straight up on her knees again, but made the mistake of looking over her shoulder. The tumbleweeds were inches away. Glitter froze. This was it. She was going to die.

"You get away from my girl, you spiky bastards!"

Glitter dragged her eyes away from the advancing tumbleweeds and spotted Dean running towards her, waving his jacket in the air like a matador's cape.

"Dean, don't!" she screamed. But when she turned back to the tumbleweeds, they'd stopped moving, almost as though they were listening to Dean.

"Yeah, you want me, don't you?" he yelled. Then, in an undertone: "*Get up, Glitz. Quick.* Yeah, it's me, the one who tricked your leader. You recognize me, don't you? *Glitz, get UP.*"

Glitter scrambled to her feet, momentarily dumbfounded by the sight of Dean facing down a wall of killer plants. Then he hissed, "Run!", and she limped down the alleyway as fast as she could.

"You want me?" Dean shouted. "Well, why don't you come get me?!"

Glitter threw a glance back to see him sprinting off in the opposite direction, still waving his jacket. She stumbled to a halt and screamed at the top of her lungs:

"Dean! Don't be an idiot! DEAN!"

But it was too late. The tumbleweeds fell on him, knocking him to the ground. He let out a howl, and Glitter, unable to watch any longer, turned away.

She fled along the sidewalk, crying and hobbling, towards Buddy and Cindy-Lou. They stood on the corner, watching in mute horror. From their horrified expressions, Glitter could guess what was happening. The sound of Dean's screams was enough.

What was worse was the silence after.

"We'd better move," Buddy said. Glitter didn't like the way he looked at her—sort of afraid, nervous, as though he didn't know what she might do next. "Come on, Glitter."

Glitter couldn't. Her legs didn't work anymore, and not because of the twisted ankle. They'd just stopped, numb. Her whole body was numb. She thought about moving, but her limbs wouldn't obey.

"Glitter." Cindy-Lou tugged on her arm, those big blue eyes welling up with tears. "Glitter, he did that to save you. They're going to come back for us soon. We have to go."

Some tiny, reactionary part of Glitter's hind brain snapped into action, and she ran, following Buddy and Cindy-Lou around the corner and along the block to the back entrance of the Peacock. She felt distant, as though she was looking down at herself from above. How could she still be moving? What was she doing it for? Surely none of it mattered anymore?

Dean's dead.

The thought flitted through her brain, and she chased it away. She didn't want that thought. She didn't want *any* thoughts. She'd just keep running and not thinking, as long as it took.

She let Buddy shove her through the employee exit of the hotel. Running and not thinking. Running and not thinking.

Dean's dead.

No. Just keep moving.

Cindy-Lou joined them in the corridor, and Buddy slammed the door shut behind them. He leaned against it, panting, sweat rolling down his face. In the hallway it was cool and quiet, and there was nowhere to run to anymore.

Dean's dead.

Glitter didn't realize she'd said it aloud until Cindy-Lou wrapped her arms around her.

"I'm so sorry!" the younger woman squeaked, burying her face in Glitter's shoulder. "I'm so, so sorry."

Glitter stood rigidly until Cindy-Lou released her.

"Are you okay? No, of course you're not okay." Cindy-Lou bit her lip, glancing over at Buddy, who looked as though he was battling to contain his impatience.

"We need to find a telephone," he said, a tremor in his voice. "We have to stop it … Glitter, how do we get to the lobby from here?"

Glitter's thoughts moved sluggishly, like swamp water. She slipped from Cindy-Lou's grip and walked down the hallway. The walls loomed in on her, bending, curving, shrinking to form a dark tunnel with no light at its end. Dean was dead. Dead. What was she going to do?

She felt a hand creep into hers. Cindy-Lou. She squeezed Glitter's fingers, walking alongside her silently. Maybe the kid was okay, after all. At least she seemed to know when to keep her mouth shut.

They emerged into the lobby. Frantic guests crowded around the gold peacock statue at its center. The receptionist in the green uniform was trying to field queries from dozens of people at once, whilst looking on the brink of tears herself.

"I don't know!" she wailed. "I'm sorry, I don't know what's happening. The police told us not to let anyone leave, that's all. I don't know anything else!"

Buddy stepped up to the desk. "Ma'am, is it possible for me to use your telephone?"

The receptionist shook her head. "Not possible."

"I work for the United States Air Force. It's extremely urgent."

"So's everything!" She turned to another hotel resident. "No, Miss, there won't be any buffet lunch today …"

"Ma'am," Buddy tried again, "I can show you my ID if that would help?"

"Will your ID reconnect the line?" the receptionist snapped. "No, I didn't think so."

"Wait, the phone lines are down?" Buddy said.

"That's what I said."

Buddy's face fell. He gripped the reception desk as though it might stop the world from crumbling around him.

Cindy-Lou touched his shoulder. "Bud? Buddy Bear? It's okay. Don't worry, we'll find another way to get hold of the base. Hey, someone's probably told them already. I'll bet they're on their way. They'll be here any minute, won't they, Glitter?"

Glitter said nothing. Dean was dead. What did any of it matter? Perhaps the cavalry would arrive. Perhaps they wouldn't, and the tumbleweeds would storm the hotel and they'd all be ripped to shreds. She didn't care anymore. Her life was in tatters, anyway. She didn't deserve to survive this. Buddy and Cindy-Lou did, sure. They were good people, with their whole lives ahead of them. They were gonna have some good kids and raise them in a nice house in a decent neighborhood, and one of them would probably grow up to be a doctor or a scientist or some sorta politician or something. Somebody important. Not like Glitter. Glitter had been born a waste of space, and she'd lived her life as a waste of space. All she knew was how to take her clothes off and hang around with shady folks.

Like Dean.

Dean.

Dean was dead.

Dean had been a drunk and a sleazeball, but he'd also been the only thing holding her together. Oh, it hadn't been much: their 'relationship' was shitty, and he'd never valued her the way he should, but he *had* valued her. She knew that now. He'd valued her enough that he'd died to save her. Nobody else would ever have done that for her. Nobody had ever loved her that way. Not her parents. Not anybody.

Her legs crumpled as a howl burst from her throat, and all the darkness she'd been holding inside spewed out, all at once.

"Glitter!" Cindy-Lou ran over. She crouched beside Glitter, pulling her close to her chest and stroking her hair like she was a baby. "Oh, it's okay. It's okay. It's gonna be fine, Glitter, you'll see. It's gonna be fine."

But it wasn't gonna be fine. Not ever, ever again.

13

Jimmy wanted cannoli. For some reason, it was all he could think about. The crunch of the pastry shell as he bit into it. The creamy sweetness of the filling. Momma used to make it with nutmeg, for extra flavor. His mouth watered. *Cannoli, just like Momma made it ...*

Then he became aware of the thumping in his skull. A sick, pulsing ache that turned his stomach and chased away all thoughts of dessert. His head rested on hard ground. He could taste blood. He wasn't entirely sure he was breathing.

"Mr. Catalano?" Somebody was shaking him. Jimmy kept his eyes tight shut, wishing they would go away. "Mr. Catalano! Are you all right?"

Jimmy groaned and opened his eyes to see his bodyguard, Al, crouched over him.

"What ... happened?" Jimmy managed. His throat was so constricted he could barely speak, and his voice sounded strange. Almost ... metallic. Frowning, he realized he couldn't remember a thing since Sergeant Valentino had shown up at the bar. Beneath the headache, there was a buzzing at the back of his skull that made his thoughts fade in and out like bad radio reception.

"Mr. Valentine choked you," said Al. The bodyguard's nose was broken. "I thought you were dead. They tied me up here, and I had to wait for Carlo to come back and let me loose."

Fzzzzt.

The radio waves inside Jimmy's head buzzed and jittered. Alien voices clamored, clicking and screeching. Jimmy pressed his hands against his ears. Pain shot through his temples, sharp as razor-wire. Clumsily, he got to his feet, feeling as though he was watching himself from a distance. His body didn't seem to belong to him. His hands and feet … He couldn't feel them. *He couldn't feel his hands.*

He turned to Al. The human was small. Fleshy. Disgusting. Everything about him turned Jimmy's stomach, from the fine red veins in his bulging eyes, to the beads of sweat that formed at his receding hairline. Al's nose hairs quivered.

"We must find them," Jimmy heard himself say. The voice—*his* voice—bounced around his head like a pinball. "They will jeopardize the mission."

"M-mission?" Al backed away.

His breathing irritated Jimmy. Sucking in all that air.

Expelling it out again, all filthy and contaminated. These humans revolted him.

He lifted a hand, pointing it at Al's chest. Watched his own soft flesh change. Harden. Solidify into a lance, shining and sharp. And then he stabbed it through Al's heart.

14

Glitter, Buddy, and Cindy-Lou sat on the white leather sofa in Dean's suite, listening to the battering of the tumble-weeds against the lobby doors below. Downstairs, there were so many of them outside that they blocked out the light, so Glitter and the others had retreated to the top floor to get a better look at what was going on. Buddy had raided Dean's mini-bar and found soft drinks and packets of pea-nuts to tide them over, considering none of them had eaten a thing since the previous night.

Glitter had no appetite, though. She sipped some soda, but couldn't even bring herself to pick at the nuts. Instead, she went to the window and gazed out at the tumbleweeds surrounding the hotel. They were like an army conducting a siege. Every so often they would fall back, only to recom-mence their barrage moments later. The steady thudding had been going on so long that it had become background noise. Relentless. Inevitable.

Not that Glitter cared. While Buddy and Cindy-Lou

muttered together on the sofa, trying to formulate a plan to escape the hotel and drive to the air base, Glitter thought about what a waste her life had been. For so many years, she'd frittered away her love like gambling chips on a man who preferred any woman but her. And even if he'd come through for her in the end, well, what of it? It didn't make up for all those years of feeling small and unimportant. Her soul felt as ragged and torn up as any of the tumbleweeds' victims.

But she would miss him.

When she started to cry, Cindy-Lou came up beside her and slipped an arm around her shaking shoulders.

"Shhh," she murmured, rubbing Glitter's arm. "It's gonna be okay. We're gonna get out of here, I promise."

"It doesn't matter," said Glitter. "Even if we get out of here, even if those … *things* … just vanish back wherever they came from, there's nothing left for me."

"Don't talk like that."

"Why the heck shouldn't I talk like that?" Glitter snapped, suddenly furious at Cindy-Lou and her pretty blue eyes. "What do you know? You've got it all sorted out, haven't you? Husband, kids, house in the suburbs … yeah, it's all gonna go swell for you, Little Miss Perfect."

Cindy-Lou recoiled.

"It's not … I—I mean, I don't …" She looked as though

she was about to cry too, and that irritated Glitter even more.

"Go on, what is it? Spit it out."

Cindy-Lou glanced towards the sofa, but Buddy was nowhere to be seen.

"I'm not perfect, that's all," she muttered.

"Oh, sure, Miss 'I'll have a soda'. What are you gonna tell me? Did you steal a lipstick once when you were in tenth grade?"

"No, not that. I …" she hesitated. "All right. If we're going to die anyway … You promise you won't tell Buddy?"

"I don't care what you get up to," Glitter replied. "Your secret's safe with me."

"All right. Well, it *was* in tenth grade, but it wasn't stealing. There was this boy … Steve, his name was. And he looked …" Cindy-Lou let out a choked laugh. "He looked like Dean Valentine! My goodness, I thought he was the biggest dreamboat I ever saw, so I let him take me to a diner for milkshakes, and after we went for a drive in his pickup. One thing led to another, and I … well …" she lowered her voice still further. "I got pregnant."

Glitter almost snorted with laughter, then bit it back when she realized the girl was serious.

"Oh," she said. "You, the preacher's daughter? That can't've gone down well with Daddy."

Cindy-Lou nodded. "I knew when my father found out

I'd be in so much trouble, and I guess I panicked. I tried—I tried—" Cindy-Lou gulped back a sob. "I tried to get it out. I knew I'd be in so much trouble! I was all by myself, and I b-bled so much I nearly died. My brother found me on the bathroom floor, and I got rushed to the hospital."

Glitter didn't speak. She didn't know what to say. She'd heard of girls who'd done similar things—in her line of work, it wasn't unusual to end up in a 'predicament'. But someone like Cindy-Lou? It didn't seem right. She rubbed the younger woman's arm, feeling awkward, as Cindy-Lou went on:

"The doctors said I can't have children," she whispered. "Not ever. So there you go. I'm not perfect. I'm damaged goods, and Buddy doesn't even know. He thinks I'm a good girl, but I'm not. I—I'm ruined."

Cindy-Lou dissolved into tears. Glitter hesitated between sympathy and exasperation, then finally pulled her into a hug.

"Hey, you're not damaged goods, you hear me? You're a good person. What happened wasn't your fault, you understand? And Buddy's lucky to have you."

"I should've known better," Cindy-Lou sobbed. She looked up at Glitter, her eyes spilling over with tears. "I'm so sorry. You were upset and now I've made it all about me."

Glitter took her hands. "Promise me you'll tell Buddy. He loves you. He'll support you."

"Do you think so?"

"I know so."

There was a pause, and Glitter frowned. Something had changed. Something she couldn't quite put her finger on.

"It's quiet," said Cindy-Lou.

That was it. There was no more thudding. Just silence. The tumbleweed barrage had stopped.

Glitter and Cindy-Lou exchanged glances.

"Do you think they've given up?" Cindy-Lou asked.

Glitter and Cindy-Lou turned to the window, looking out at the Peacock's parking lot. Silent, still tumbleweeds covered the ground and most of the cars. The sun blazed overhead. Nothing moved. Nothing made a sound. It was eerie.

"What's it doing?" Glitter whispered.

Cindy-Lou didn't answer. She only raised her hand and pointed. And then Glitter saw it. A lone, dark figure, walking right up the center of the strip. A figure in a pinstripe suit and a fedora, making a beeline for the hotel, tumbleweeds parting ahead of him like the Red Sea.

It was Jimmy.

15

Cindy-Lou stared through the window at the approaching figure of Jimmy the Shark. Somehow, that one man seemed more frightening to her than all the tumbleweed-aliens combined, but despite her fear, all she could think about was her secret. She wasn't sure what had made her tell Glitter, except that she'd held it in so long that she'd needed to tell *somebody*. But now it felt so much more real, the weight of it bearing down on her just like Jimmy was. She gripped the windowsill, stiffening when Buddy put his arm around her.

"Where did you go?" she asked him.

"Out to the landing. I could see better from the window there." He squeezed her shoulder. "It'll be all right. I'll think of something."

Cindy-Lou slipped out of his embrace. She couldn't bear to look at him. She loved Buddy—really loved him—but she'd always kept a part of herself closed off from him. The hard, calcified shell that had formed around her secret.

It had been easy to forget about it during the heady days

of wedding planning, when she'd been full of hopes and dreams for the future, but now he was the only person in the room who didn't know what she'd done, she began to understand that it would always be there. The secret held her apart from him, black and malignant like a cancer.

She knew he dreamed of a family. Two kids, a boy and a girl. He'd even talked about what they would name them: Buddy Jr. and little Betty-May. She knew when he closed his eyes he could see them playing in the backyard with their dog, while he stoked up the barbecue and she passed out drinks to their friends.

How could she tell him he would never have that? Not now he'd shackled himself to her. Glitter was right—she ought to tell him and face the consequences, whatever they may be.

But not now. Right now, they had to focus on surviving.

Jimmy reached the Peacock's parking lot and stopped, looking up at the hotel. Cindy-Lou shrank back from the window when his gaze ventured their way.

"What does he want with us?" she whispered.

Buddy let out a heavy sigh.

"It's me he wants," he said. "I let slip that I work on the air base. That we were investigating an object that fell from the sky." A look of distress crossed his face. "I had no idea who—or rather *what*—I was talking to when I said that.

Now it knows we've been holding the other craft captive, and I'm betting it wants back what we've taken. Perhaps that's the reason it came here in the first place." He took a long breath. "I have to go out there and talk to it."

"Buddy Bear ..." Cindy-Lou began.

"No, don't try to talk me out of it. It wants me, not everybody else in this hotel, but it'll kill everyone to reach me if it has to. I can't let that happen."

"Buddy, you can't! You don't know all that!"

Buddy took her hands. "I have no choice. I'm sure I'm right. I love you, Cindy-Lou. I'll come back to you, I promise."

Cindy-Lou blinked back tears. "You better not break your promise, Buddy Hitchcock. You just better not!"

16

An expectant hush permeated the lobby. A small knot of people, the receptionist amongst them, stood at the glass doors looking out at the parking lot. The rest hung back, watching from what they obviously hoped was a safe distance. Buddy forced his way to the front of the crowd, followed by Glitter and Cindy-Lou.

In the parking lot, surrounded by a semi-circular wall of tumbleweeds over ten feet high, stood Jimmy the Shark. His eyes glowed silver, and even his skin had taken on a shiny, waxen appearance. Buddy put one hand on the golden 'PH' door handle and paused for a breath to summon his courage. But fear was only one of the emotions that raced through him as he pushed the door open.

What stood in that parking lot was an alien being: there was barely a trace of the real Jimmy left, judging by its eerie stillness and the way its eyes flickered as it watched Buddy cross the asphalt. Natural scientific curiosity kept Buddy moving despite his nerves, not to mention pride at the thought of being the first man to speak to an extra-terrestrial visitor. What might he learn if he survived this encounter? What stories might he be able to tell?

For an instant, an image of him and Cindy-Lou shaking hands with the President flashed through his mind, and then he was standing right in front of Jimmy, so close they could have touched, and all his silly fantasies slipped off him like an unneeded skin, leaving only the two of them. Buddy and the alien. They looked at each other, and there might as well have been nothing and nobody else in the world. The afternoon heat was suffocating, making him catch his breath.

"Are you the envoy?" said Jimmy. The wiry tumbleweed wall around him acted as an amplifier, projecting his voice out into the parking lot.

"I—Yes. I suppose so." Buddy's mouth was dry. "Why are you here? What do you want?"

"We want what was taken from us."

"The craft that crash landed."

The silver in Jimmy's eyes swirled. "You will take us to it."

Buddy swallowed. "I—I can't do that. But if you let me contact my superiors, I'll …"

"We do not require your obedience. Only your information."

Jimmy lifted his arm. Buddy's eyes widened. His skin

was … it was *melting.* The silvery flesh flowed over itself, becoming viscous in consistency. Buddy frowned. How did it achieve this? It seemed to be changing the make-up of Jimmy's body at an atomic level. He imagined millions upon millions of tiny, self-sufficient particles flooding Jimmy's bloodstream, latching onto his cells, altering them—

Buddy let out a strangled cry as something ensnared his throat. His feet left the ground, and he looked down to see Jimmy's semi-liquid hand clamped around his neck. Icy prickles crawled over his skin like tiny spider legs. The sensation spread down Buddy's chest and arms, up to his head, cold spiders creeping over his skull, into his eyes, his nose, his mouth. He couldn't see. Couldn't breathe. Couldn't speak. Couldn't hear, except for one thing: Jimmy's echoing voice, ringing clear as a radio broadcast through his skull.

Take us to our craft.

17

"Buddy!"

Cindy-Lou flung open the hotel doors and ran out into the parking lot. Glitter followed, unable to tear her eyes away from the sight of Buddy suspended in the air. A stream of molten silver flowed from Jimmy's arm, enveloping Buddy from head to toe, and all they could do was watch in horror as it consumed his entire body.

"Buddy! No! Stop, please! Let him go!"

Glitter caught up with Cindy-Lou just in time, grabbing her by the waist before she could throw herself at Buddy's captor. For a moment, Cindy-Lou struggled, but Glitter held fast, and eventually the newlywed grew still, her chest heaving with sobs.

The wall of tumbleweeds crumbled, reforming into a wave that engulfed both Buddy and Jimmy.

"What's happening?" Cindy-Lou wailed. "Buddy! What has it done to Buddy?!" She tried to bolt again, and Glitter clung tighter.

"Don't! You don't know what'll happen to you if you go near it."

"I don't care! It's taken Buddy. Let me go. Let me go!"

The tumbleweeds flowed away like fast-moving lava. Every stray tumbleweed in the area joined the surge, swelling it ever bigger as it rolled down the strip and out of town, leaving nothing but destruction in its wake.

"Looks like it's headed for the air base," Glitter said.

"We have to follow it," Cindy-Lou replied. "We have to save Buddy."

Glitter wondered whether there was anything left of Buddy to save. As the flood of tumbleweeds vanished into the distance, she scanned the empty parking lot. Most of the cars had been crushed or broken, and the vast Peacock sign hung off its hinges, neon lights spluttering. But somehow, miraculously, Dean's sea-green Cadillac remained unharmed. It sat in pride of place close to the door, as pristine and gleaming as ever.

Typical, Glitter thought, and almost smiled. Then she bit her lip, choking back tears.

"Come on." She took Cindy-Lou's hand and hurried over to the car. "If we go now, we might still catch up."

Glitter found the car keys in the glove compartment, and soon the Cadillac growled to life. Cindy-Lou grabbed the door handle as Glitter sped off down the strip, swerving shredded bodies and abandoned cars.

Cindy-Lou yelled something that Glitter couldn't quite catch over the roar of the engine.

"What's that?" she shouted back.

"I said you drive like a maniac!"

Glitter allowed her the briefest of glances before returning her eyes to the road. "Thought you wanted to catch up to them?"

"I do, but …"

"But nothing." Glitter put her foot to the floor as they shot out of town. "Shut up and let me drive."

It felt good to be moving again. The wind in her hair blew away all her cares, all her doubts. Dean was dead, and that was an ache in her chest that might never go away, but she was here, she was alive, she was *doing something.* But just as they were on the brink of catching up to the plants, something caught her eye. She slowed the car.

"Wait, what are you doing?" Cindy-Lou stared off into the distance, where the tumbleweeds were vanishing over the horizon like a distant sandstorm. "We're going to lose them."

Glitter swerved off the highway and took the Cadillac off-road, bumping along the sand in the direction of the silvery gleam. When Cindy-Lou spotted what they were headed for, she leaned forward, staring through the windscreen.

"Is that …?"

"Yes," said Glitter. "I think it's the second craft. The one that Jimmy found."

The Cadillac wasn't made for off-roading. Every tiny rock or dip in the landscape caused the car to lurch and sway. Glitter gripped the wheel, battling to keep it under control.

"But what about Buddy?" Cindy-Lou protested.

"What were we gonna do if we caught up with him?" Glitter replied. "Perhaps we can find something to help us here. Some clue how to defeat those things."

She brought the Cadillac to a halt just a few meters shy of the gleaming silver disc. It lay half-embedded in a crater, dust and dirt kicked up all around. Glitter slipped out of the driver's seat and crept towards it, soon becoming aware of Cindy-Lou alongside her.

"I wish Buddy were here," Cindy-Lou whispered. "He'd know what to do."

"Well, he ain't." Glitter was aware she sounded harsher than she meant to be. "It's just us. So what do you think?" She stopped at the edge of the crater. "How do we get into it?"

"*Into* it?" Cindy-Lou looked at Glitter, then back at the crater. Glitter gave a little shrug.

The disc was smooth and featureless. There was nothing whatsoever to indicate an opening. It looked a little like a silver spinning top Glitter'd had as a child. To think this thing had flown through outer space from some distant alien planet.

She started down the slope, carefully, trying to ignore the pain flaring in her ankle. She'd probably never dance again after this. Not for a good while, at least. The vision of a future standing at the craps tables swam into her mind, and she figured she had nothing much to lose.

The atmosphere grew hotter the closer she got to the craft. At first she thought it was just the sun, but then she realized that the disc itself was giving off warmth. There was a tang to the surrounding air. An anticipation. It was almost as if it were … alive.

"Don't touch it!"

Glitter looked over her shoulder to see Cindy-Lou stumbling down the slope, barefoot. She'd slipped off her pumps and left them on the edge of the crater. For the first time, she looked less than pristine, her dark hair sticking to her forehead, her face smeared with dust.

"You better not touch it," she repeated breathlessly, coming to a halt beside Glitter. "We don't know what we're dealing with. Think what it did to Jimmy."

Glitter crept up to the craft and peered at its smooth,

featureless surface, then made a slow circuit around it, examining every part that wasn't buried beneath the sand.

"Well?" Cindy-Lou said, when she returned.

"I can't see a thing." Glitter stepped back. "Not a crack anywhere. No way in. But those things got out of it somehow. It must have an opening. Perhaps they communicate with it somehow. Open it with a word, or even a thought …"

Nervously, she brushed her fingers against the metal casing. Nothing happened. She pressed her palm flat on it and winced. It was hot to the touch. She pulled her hand away. Still nothing.

"Buddy said the alien substance was a kind of metal," she mused. She reached into the pocket of her shorts and withdrew her lighter—stainless steel, engraved with her real name. The only proper present Dean had ever given her. She held it up to show Cindy-Lou.

"Do you think …?"

Cindy-Lou nodded. "Try it."

Glitter pressed the lighter to the metal surface with a *clink*. Immediately, she felt ridiculous.

"Oh, this is stupid," she said, clutching the lighter in her palm. "It's never going to open for us."

"Glitter?"

Glitter turned at the sound of the familiar voice and

squinted up at the rim of the crater. Two figures—one lanky, one squat—stood shrouded in shadow, the afternoon sun low behind them. She put a hand to her eyes, trying to make out the faces.

"Paulo?"

"Say, fancy seeing you here." The lanky one, Paulo, stumbled his way down the slope, his face breaking into an oversized grin. "You're looking swell, Glitter. Buy you a drink?"

"That some kinda joke?" Glitter glanced at Cindy-Lou, who looked equally bemused. "How'd you get here, Paulo?"

A puzzled look passed across his face. "I—don't remember."

The other figure, the squat one, followed his fellow mobster into the crater. He was another of Jimmy's guys, Glitter realized. Larry? Luca? Something like that. Coming to a halt just behind Paulo, he lifted his gun, pointing it at Paulo's head. Glitter's hands flew to her mouth.

"P—"

Click.

Click. Click. Click.

The gun was empty. There were no rounds left. Still, Luca kept pressing the trigger. *Click, click, click.* Paulo didn't even seem to notice. A queasy feeling washed over

Glitter's stomach.

"Paulo," she said. "How did you get here? What happened?"

"Say, you're looking swell, Glitter. Buy you a drink?"

He smiled broadly. Too broadly, until it looked as though his face might split. His eyes shone silver. He reached out his arms toward Glitter, grabbing for her, and she screamed.

Glitter dodged Paulo's lunge and he fell against the spacecraft, yelping when his hands made contact with the hot surface. He whirled round, grabbing at her, and Glitter did the only thing she could think to do. She lifted the lighter and flicked it on, shoving the flame straight into Paulo's face. He stumbled back, letting out a high-pitched squeal like radio feedback. Luca lumbered toward her in his place, and Glitter turned the lighter on him, gesturing for Cindy-Lou to get behind her.

"What are you doing?" Cindy-Lou squeaked.

"They're afraid of fire," Glitter hissed. "Stay behind me!"

As Glitter held off the mobsters with the flickering lighter flame, Cindy-Lou scooped up a dry branch from the ground and shoved it into Glitter's hands.

"Quick, light this."

Glitter held the lighter to the tip of one of the branches,

sending it up in flames, and waved it at the mobsters. They backed up, staring at the fire as though they'd never seen such a thing before. But the flames quickly engulfed the dry wood, and Glitter was forced to drop it before it singed her fingers.

"Say, Glitter, you're looking swell." Paulo lumbered towards her. Narrowly swerving his clumsy embrace, she stumbled and fell against Cindy-Lou, who spun her around, pointing.

"Glitter, look!"

There was a long, dark crack in the saucer's smooth, silver surface. It spread down the surface of the spacecraft, opening like a gaping mouth.

"Buy you a drink?" Paulo asked and shoved both the girls inside.

18

The Unity was one with Buddy, and Buddy was one with the Unity.

It spread for miles, a network of senses and thoughts and minds. Hundreds. No, thousands, at least. Buddy's ears were full of their clamor, all their thoughts jostling for his attention at once. The pain of the dead and dying back in Las Vegas. Their cries. Fears. Longings. All of them so empty and full of want, trying to quench a hunger that could not be sated.

The Unity would fill that hole. They were but empty vessels, awaiting its command. Jimmy had been easy—a willing soldier, trained to follow orders without question. And there were other easy ones. The drunks. The gamblers. The down-and-outs. Desperate men and women whose only thought was to consume. Fleshy sacks, stuffing down food and alcohol. Grubbing for coins to feed into their slot machines. Filthy things, stinking of sweat and lust. The Unity despised them.

Buddy despised them. Dean Valentine, that sleaze with his cigars and whiskey, trying to hit on Buddy's wife. Trying to devour her in order to satisfy his gaping void, as if that would ever work. As if she wasn't just one of many. A conveyor belt of willing girls, delivered to his door.

And Glitter—she was just as bad. She'd helped Valentine, hadn't she? Tried to distract Buddy so Dean could get his claws into Cindy-Lou. They deserved to be destroyed.

They all did.

Buddy's body as he'd known it was gone, his essence carried along by the wave. Through the awareness of the Unity, he became conscious of their arrival at the gates of the air base. Dimly, he recognized the men guarding the entrance, as the tumbleweeds swarmed them. Soon they too, and all their knowledge, would be part of the Unity.

The Unity found the tumbleweeds a useful shape. Light, quick, easy to replicate. What it lacked in heft it made up for with invulnerability. Bullets ripped through the swarm of plants, and the Unity barely noticed.

It stormed the base, sweeping through every doorway, along every corridor, down every flight of stairs until it found the aircraft hangar where Buddy and his team had imprisoned the first spacecraft. This silver orb, crippled and chained, was the hub through which the Unity's communications with the home planet were relayed. Now it had been rendered useless by a jamming signal, the Unity was adrift, cut off from its instructions, lost without any sense of purpose. Or had been, until Buddy had let slip the spacecraft's location.

Buddy understood all of this as his feet touched the ground once more. He stepped out from the mass of tumbleweeds, his body re-forming just the same as it had been, but better. Stronger. More powerful. He flexed his fingers and walked straight through the security checkpoint. The soldiers who tried to stop him were swiftly assimilated into the Unity.

And there was more: as the Unity ripped through the base, devouring everything in its path, it discovered information it hadn't even known to look for. Passwords. Cyphers. Access codes. It learned about the Cold War, about the USSR. About the atomic bomb.

By the time Buddy reached the spacecraft, which was grounded on a plinth in the midst of a bank of computers, the Unity had almost forgotten about its original mission. There was so much more that could be done. So many resources for the taking. Greedily, it imagined the Earth itself in its clutches, every human brain at its disposal, doing its bidding. And the Bomb ... an unexpected boon. A jackpot win.

Buddy laughed. A jackpot win. How apt. He—*the*

Unity—was learning. He approached the control panel, ready to enter the password that would disable the signal jammers and allow the Unity to contact its home planet once more.

And stopped.

A wave of emotion caught him off guard. A thought, tiny amongst the clamor of human brains, calling for him in the distance. Growing louder. Stronger. Calling his name. He hesitated, his hand hovering over the control panel.

Cindy-Lou.

She was looking for him. She had been following him. Wanted to rescue him, to bring him back to himself. To her. He felt the love that bound them, wrapping itself round his heart like a velvet ribbon, tight and warm, despite their distance. Despite everything. Cindy-Lou. He forced his thoughts into some kind of clarity. If he could sense her thoughts, the Unity must have her, which meant … which meant she was in danger. He had to turn back. Had to find her.

But she lied to you.

The Unity whispered to him, intruding into his thoughts. He tried to shake it off, but it could see everything. It *knew* everything.

And it showed him.

19

The Unity invaded Cindy-Lou, tendrils snaking into her mind, transporting her back into her worst memory as she lay in the spacecraft. Pain gripped her, twisting her like two hands trying to wring all the blood from her body.

She screamed, but there was no one to hear. She'd chosen this. Chosen a night when she would be alone, when her parents were out of state, her brother was sleeping over at a friend's. She hadn't wanted to be disturbed. She didn't want anyone finding out. How could she admit to them that their golden girl had gotten herself in such a state?

But the pain—oh Lord, the pain. It was God punishing her. She deserved to be punished. She lay on the white-tiled bathroom floor and watched the blood seep through her nightgown, feeling numb and light-headed. Like a doll. Like it was happening to somebody else.

A pretty doll. Her father liked to dress her up and have her sit at the front of the congregation when he gave his sermons. She sat next to her mother and her little brother with her hands clasped in front of her, like a good girl.

But she wasn't a good girl, was she? She'd been weak. She'd let her boyfriend drive her to the make-out spot, because that was what the other girls talked about doing, and she'd let him put his hands all over her, and what was worse, she'd wanted him to. She'd wanted it. Asked for it, even. Like a common tramp, her mother would've said, if she knew. And this was her punishment. The blood and the pain.

Eve's curse, she thought, just before she passed out.

20

"Glitz? Hey, Glitter?"

The voice broke through Glitter's groggy half-dreams. Oh, how she'd longed to hear that voice—it was like a cool drink of water to a parched woman. She rolled over. The floor beneath her was hard and cold. It lurched as she moved, making her feel as though she was about to fall.

"Dean?"

She dared to open her eyes. The world swam in a haze of misty grays. She couldn't make out a thing other than the dark figure crouched beside her. He held out a hand and pulled her up to sitting, his warm fingers wrapped around hers. Glitter burst into tears.

"I thought you were dead!" She threw her arms around his neck, and Dean hugged her back, curling his fingers into her hair.

"I don't die that easy," he murmured. "Japs found that out the hard way."

"But how did you find me?" Glitter pulled back. After

what had happened, she'd expected to see him all torn up, his shirt hanging off him in shreds, but he looked pristine. Not a hair out of place, almost as though he were about to go on stage. "Where even *are* we? I remember the space-craft, and then ..."

"It's okay. Don't worry about a thing. You're safe." Dean got to his feet and helped her up. "Are you ready?"

"Ready for what?"

"The show."

Glitter looked down and realized she was wearing her showgirl costume. Suddenly, she could feel the weight of her feather headdress on her head. And now the mist was clearing, the theater emerged around her: backstage, just as she'd always known it, with her fellow dancers warming up and the sound of an excited crowd just beyond the curtain.

"No." She frowned. "This ain't right."

"C'mon, Glitz. The audience won't wait forever. Hey, look, I'm sorry, all right? I treated you bad. You didn't de-serve that. You've always been there for me. I see that now."

He cupped her chin in his hand. He was so handsome. It was just like a scene from one of his movies.

"I love you, Glitz," he said. "I always have. Give me an-other chance."

Happiness bubbled up inside her chest, then exploded in

a shower of sparks. He was telling the truth. She could feel it. She *knew*. But how did she know? There was something … something she remembered. Him shouting. Telling her to run, to save herself. And the tumbleweeds, bearing down on him.

"No … No, Dean. You died. You died!"

"You don't need to worry about that now, Glitz. We can be together. C'mon. The show's about to start."

"No." Glitter backed away. "No, this ain't right. I can't …"

The theater faded. Glitter stood in an empty room with metallic walls. The spacecraft. She was barefoot again, in her ragged shorts and blouse. But Dean was still there. Still perfect.

"You're like Paulo and Luca," she said sadly, touching his chest. "An echo."

"C'mon, Glitz." Dean smiled his broad Hollywood smile. "The show's about to start."

21

She lied to you.

Buddy knew if he switched off the signal jammer, it would all be over. Right now, the Unity was crippled, doing its best to figure out how to survive without its central mainframe. But if it could reconnect with its home planet, it would be able to contact its superiors for help. Its confused thoughts screamed through his head, an endless, screeching babble, pushing him to do its bidding.

She lied to you.

That was true. Buddy knew it was true. The Unity wasn't lying to him—it had gotten the information directly from Cindy-Lou. He'd seen it all through her own eyes—her parking up at the make-out spot with Steve. Letting him put his hand up under her petticoats. Lying on the bathroom floor weeks later, blood everywhere.

She's not what you thought she was.

Everything they'd imagined. Everything they'd dreamed about. She'd let him talk about their future kids and nodded along, all the while knowing it wasn't possible. A burning anger seared through him, and with it came visions of mushroom clouds, people running. Screaming. He could destroy them all. He had the power.

He hovered his hand over the control panel, ready to enter the access code. The crescendo of voices grew louder. Images of his false past, his ruined future, flashed through his mind like scattered Polaroids.

She lied. Kill her. Kill them all.

Cindy-Lou on their wedding day, smiling. False. Cindy-Lou holding a baby that would never come. Lies. Cindy-Lou by the pool with Dean Valentine, her idol, as he leaned in to kiss her—

Except she hadn't let him, had she?

Buddy saw it now through his wife's eyes.

"Mr. Valentine! I'm married!"

She'd worshipped Dean Valentine ever since she was a little girl. Buddy had seen the posters all over her bedroom wall. And yet, when she'd had her chance, she hadn't taken it.

Turn the dial. Kill them all.

Buddy's hand shook.

"Now, if you'll excuse me, I'm going to find my husband."

A future without her would be no future at all.

"If you don't bet," Buddy muttered, "you'll never win."

He pulled his hand away from the control panel … just as the cells of his body shut down, and he crumpled to the ground.

Jimmy the Shark stepped over him and approached the computer.

22

The floor shuddered under Glitter's feet. She wobbled and would've fallen if Dean hadn't put out his arms to catch her. A rumble started deep in the guts of the spacecraft. Judging by the way the craft rocked and swayed, they had begun to move.

Glitter whirled around, searching for some way to stop it, but there was nothing to see. No blinking lights, no controls. Just smooth, featureless metal curving all around them. Against one wall, curled up in a fetal position, lay Cindy-Lou. Glitter ran to her.

"Cindy? Cindy, can you hear me? Are you all right?"

Cindy-Lou let out a whimper and curled up even tighter. Glitter shook her.

"Cindy! Come on, wake up. We're moving. You have to help me!"

Slowly, Cindy-Lou opened her eyes. She squinted at Glitter, puzzled at first, then with dawning recognition. She sat up, and her gaze fell on Dean.

"It's not really him," Glitter said, quietly. "He's one of them now."

"C'mon Glitz." Dean beamed, his eyes glowing silver. "The show's about to start."

"Where is it taking us?" Cindy-Lou asked.

"I'm gonna venture a guess that we're going to the air base," Glitter replied. "Perhaps it's reconnected with its missing craft."

"Buddy," whispered Cindy-Lou.

She stared up at Dean, and Glitter knew exactly what she was thinking. Was Buddy no more than an echo now, too? Could what had happened to him—and Dean, and the others—be reversed?

It didn't take long for the spacecraft to reach its destination. No sooner had the rocking and swaying begun, than they were slowing down again, and before long, with a sudden drop and a lurch, they came to a halt. Glitter and Cindy-Lou looked at each other.

"Show's about to start." Dean placed a hand on the wall.

The area around his palm glowed, and the crack began to open again. As soon as it was wide enough, Dean stepped out, and Glitter and Cindy-Lou followed.

They were outside an aircraft hangar. It had grown dark while they were in the spacecraft, and stars twinkled in the night sky. All around them, in a semi-circle, stood figures with shining eyes, like an eerie welcoming committee. Glitter recognized military uniforms and showgirl costumes, the receptionist from the Peacock, and the two tourists who'd been in a hurry to catch their plane. Everyone the tumbleweeds had attacked was here: restored, renewed, and assimilated. Even the people Glitter was sure had been beyond saving had somehow been put back together, just like new. And there were more coming, still, spilling through the gates of the air base—an endless parade of zombie refugees.

Glitter felt a small hand slip into hers and looked round to see Cindy-Lou, white-faced and trembling. She squeezed the younger woman's hand.

"It's gonna be okay," she said, trying to fake a confidence she didn't feel. "It's gonna be fine."

Dean walked toward the open door of the aircraft hangar. Glitter could see nothing in the blackness beyond. She and Cindy-Lou followed Dean, and from the shadows a vast shape emerged: the captured craft, bigger and even more imposing than the one they'd just traveled in. It was a perfect silver sphere, secured to a plinth with rigging and surrounded by six-foot-tall computer banks, like the ones Glitter had seen in science fiction movies.

Cindy-Lou gasped.

"Buddy!"

She let go of Glitter's hand and ran to where her husband

lay collapsed on the ground near the craft. Jimmy stood beside him, bent over some part of the computer Glitter couldn't quite see.

"Buddy?" Cindy-Lou shook her husband's shoulder. "Buddy?"

"He won't wake." Jimmy's voice rang out through the hangar.

Cindy-Lou looked up in horror. "Is he … dead?"

"He was no longer useful to us." Jimmy turned back to the control panel. Glitter tried to approach Cindy-Lou as she crouched, weeping, over her husband, but was stopped by Dean's hand on her shoulder.

"We will contact our home planet," Dean said. "Something is disabling our network. We need the scientist's access codes." He looked down at Cindy-Lou. "You will help us."

Cindy-Lou scowled through her tears. "Never!"

Dean let go of Glitter and walked over to Buddy. He crouched and put a hand to Buddy's forehead. Buddy's eyes flicked open like a doll's. He sat up. Cindy-Lou scurried back and stared at him, dumbfounded, but Dean picked her up by the hair, wrenching her to her feet. His arm shimmered, growing sharp and metallic, and he held the blade to Cindy-Lou's throat.

"Tell us the access codes," Dean said, as Cindy-Lou

whimpered, her eyes wide and terrified, "or this one will die."

Glitter's mind raced. The aliens could control anyone they liked, or so it seemed, but they hadn't been able to control Buddy. Why? The answer must've had something to do with Cindy-Lou, otherwise why would they have brought her here?

Realization dawned in Glitter's mind like a bright neon light. Echoes. The aliens couldn't override everything about their human hosts. They hadn't been able to prevent Jimmy from acting according to his military instincts. They couldn't stop Buddy from loving Cindy-Lou. He must've fought against them, to save her.

And if that was the case, then maybe, just maybe …

Glitter rooted around in her pocket. Yes! Still there.

"Dean," she called. "Catch!"

Acting on reflex, as she'd hoped, Dean let go of Cindy-Lou in order to catch the lighter. He looked down at it, momentarily puzzled.

"Do you remember?" Glitter asked him, taking a few nervous steps in his direction. "You took me out to the Grand Canyon. It was the one time you took me anywhere, and we had such a good time. Do you remember? And in the little gift shop, you bought me that. You had it engraved with my name. Look, see?"

She was close enough now to point to the engraving: *Margaret.*

"That's me," she whispered, looking up at him hopefully. "Margaret. I know you cared about me. You cared enough to sacrifice your life for me back there in Vegas, remember? Dean?"

Dean's blank expression wavered. The silver light in his eyes seemed to dim.

"Margaret," he murmured.

"I never let you down, did I, Dean? I stood by you, thick and thin. Come back to me now."

A scream sliced the air. Cindy-Lou. Glitter turned to see Jimmy bearing down on her, brandishing one of his knife-like arms.

"We require the access codes."

Cindy-Lou tried to run, tripped, and fell on Buddy, who stared at her with dawning recognition.

"Cindy?"

He looked up at Jimmy in horror and tried to pull Cindy-Lou out of the mobster's path, but the two of them were backed up against the control panel. There was nowhere for them to go. Then Jimmy stopped. His body jerked. Silvery blood poured from his mouth.

Dean withdrew his sharpened arm from Jimmy's chest.

"I never liked that guy," he said, as Jimmy crumpled to

the floor.

23

"Dean?" Glitter hung back nervously as his arm shrunk to its normal state. "Are you okay? Is it really you?"

"Beats me." Dean stared at his hand, turning it over with a look of bemusement. "How the heck did I do that? What's going on? I don't remember a thing since we were in the alley with all those damn weeds."

"It really *is* you." Glitter blinked back tears, turning her head so he wouldn't see.

As she did, she caught sight of Cindy-Lou and Buddy. They were on their feet now, hand-in-hand, staring out at the hangar entrance. Moonlight poured in, casting a silver sheen over the frozen expressions of horror on their faces.

No, not moonlight.

Not at all.

Glitter stepped back, clutching at Dean's arm as the silver light moved closer, and shifted, shadowy forms appearing out of the brightness. The glow was coming from dozens, maybe hundreds of pairs of eyes. The zombies shuffled forward, slowly but relentlessly, fixed on their destination. The spacecraft.

"They're coming!" Glitter hissed. "We have to stop them!"

"Wait, I can do this." Buddy turned to the control panel. "I can extend the range of the radio jammer and block the Unity from communicating with its units. I just need time to find the right frequency for their network."

Glitter and the others backed up close to him as the zombies closed in. The only sounds in the hangar were the shuffling of zombie feet, and the squeal of feedback as Buddy adjusted the radio's knobs.

"You have to be quick!" Glitter told him.

"Just a moment longer." Sweat beaded on Buddy's brow. "Hold them off."

"How are we supposed to do that?!" Cindy-Lou cried.

The zombies were almost on them. The eerie silver glow lit up the hangar. One of them reached out his arms, his fingers almost grazing Glitter's shoulder.

"Fire!" she shouted. "They're scared of fire! Dean, the lighter!"

Dean flicked on the lighter and held it at arm's length, waving the tiny flame from side to side. The zombies drew to a halt, watching. Glitter dug her nails into her palms, knowing they only had a few seconds, if that. There had to be something else here that they could burn.

Then she saw it: a petrol canister tucked behind the control panel. She ducked past Buddy and grabbed it, unscrewing the lid just as the nearest zombie knocked the lighter from Dean's hand.

The lighter fell, and Glitter tipped the canister on its side, sending gasoline spewing across the hangar floor. The spill went up in flames, so close the heat singed her eyelashes.

But the zombies were forced to back up, and it was enough. Buddy jumped away from the console, letting out a whoop.

"Got it!" He grabbed Glitter and Cindy-Lou's hands, and they all rushed behind the computer, out of reach of the flames. On the other side of the wall of fire, the zombies shuddered, trembled, dropped to the floor as their connection with the Unity was severed. Silence fell over the hangar, broken only by the crackle of the fire as it flared and burned out.

"Will they be okay?" Cindy-Lou whispered, peering out from behind the console at the sea of bodies.

"I think so," said Buddy. "Now that the Unity has no way to control them, they should return to themselves in time."

Sure enough, people were already stirring. They sat up, rubbing their eyes, looking puzzled. Relief flooded Glitter's veins.

"We're okay." She leaned her head back against the console. "We did it. We're okay."

24

That night, soldiers arrived with flame-throwers to round up the tumbleweeds. Like shepherds herding sheep, they gathered the plants—now adrift and fearful without the Unity's instructions—into neat piles on the runway and incinerated them. Clouds of smoke spiraled into the dark sky, obscuring the stars.

Buddy stood on the grass verge and watched as the last vestiges of Earth's only contact with an alien civilization burned. The two spacecraft, along with Jimmy the Shark's silver-smeared corpse, were hefted onto an unmarked truck and taken away. Nobody would tell him where.

Meanwhile, the people who'd been affected by the Unity's control seemed to recover their usual selves. More than that: they emerged from the experience with their injuries healed, and, as they were taken one-by-one through a lengthy examination and debrief in one of the aircraft hangars, some even reported higher than usual levels of energy and strength. Preliminary blood tests, however, showed no further anomalies, and after signing a document swearing them to secrecy, the civilians were allowed to return home.

As the sun rose, Buddy and the others rode in the back of a military transport, heading for Las Vegas. Their journey was a silent one, for the most part. Buddy had been given leave to return to his honeymoon, which he took gladly, keen to stay by Cindy-Lou's side for as long as possible. He'd come close to losing her that night, and he could feel his priorities shifting. The future he'd once imagined was not the one that now stretched ahead of him. And that, he thought, as he watched his wife turn to fix her eyes on the horizon, the wind blowing her hair around her dirt-smeared face, was all right with him.

Along the way, they spotted Dean's car abandoned at the crash site. Dean shouted to the driver to make a stop, and they pulled over to where Paulo and Luca sat, confused, at the side of the road.

"Gotta take my baby home." Dean jumped out of the transport, his eyes on the car. He glanced back at Glitter, who took his hand with a shy smile and let him help her to the ground. She hadn't said much since things had calmed down, but Buddy had noticed her gazing at Dean as though she couldn't quite believe her luck. He supposed it was pretty crazy—the guy had died and come back to life, after all.

"Catch up with us when you get back," he said.

"Sure thing." Dean nodded, and he and Glitter walked off toward the Cadillac, while the soldiers helped the befuddled Paulo and Luca into the transport.

Paulo rubbed his eyes and squinted, looking around as though he'd just woken up and couldn't quite work out whether he was still dreaming.

"What the heck happened?" he asked.

Buddy shook his head. "You wouldn't believe me if I told you."

※:※:※:※:※:※:※

After a few hours' sleep, the four of them reunited in Dean's suite. Buddy and Cindy-Lou stood at the window, arms around one another's waists, looking out at the decimated remains of the city. Dean lounged on the sofa, while Glitter fixed some drinks.

"What can I get y'all?" she asked, looking at Cindy-Lou. "Soda?"

Cindy-Lou let out a long breath, glancing over her shoulder.

"Gee, Glitter, I think I'm gonna need something stronger than that, after everything we've been through. What was it you said? 'This is Vegas, Baby Doll … '"

"… we don't do temperance." A smile spread across Glitter's face. "Vodka martini it is, then. Say, Dean, how about you put on a record?"

Dean rose, stretched, and shuffled over to the record player, out of earshot. Glitter passed Cindy-Lou and Buddy their drinks, and leaned in close to them.

"You guys gonna be okay?" she asked, her eyes on Cindy-Lou's face.

Cindy-Lou smiled, looking up at her husband. "I think so. We were talking on the way back to the city. We thought we might do something different, you know?"

Buddy nodded. "Cindy's always wanted to travel, haven't you? So we figured, after all the debriefing is done, I'll quit my job at the base and we'll go to Europe. Paris first, isn't that right, Cindy?"

"Sure is!" Cindy-Lou beamed. "And you, Glitter? What are you going to do?"

Glitter looked down at her ankle, which the army paramedics had bandaged up. "Well, I'm afraid my dancing days are over, at least for the time being."

Cindy-Lou put a hand on her arm. "Hey, I'm sorry."

"No, don't be. There's only so long a girl can go on high kicking, really. And Dean and I had a little talk." She smiled, shyly. "He's making a new movie next year, and he thinks I'd be perfect in the lead role."

Cindy-Lou's eyes widened. "You're gonna be an *actress*? Glitter, that's amazing!" She clapped her hands, then threw her arms around Glitter's neck. Glitter laughed, momentarily startled, then returned the hug, looking over Cindy-Lou's shoulder at Buddy, who raised his glass with a smile.

"Congratulations, Glitter."

"Thank you." Glitter broke from the hug just as music rang through the suite: a tune that was as familiar to her as her own name. One of Dean's. She laughed. Suddenly, it really did seem like everything was gonna be fine.

You and me girl / We're just tumbleweeds driftin' in the breeze.

"Seriously, Dean? This one?" she said, as Dean strolled over, cigar in hand.

Dean shrugged. "Seemed appropriate." He turned to a nearby table and picked up the phone. "Hey, I'm gonna order room service. You folks want anything?"

"Sure thing," said Cindy-Lou.

Buddy nodded. "I could eat a horse."

"Reckon I'll go straight to dessert." Dean frowned at the menu. "I don't know why, but I've got this mean craving for cannoli."

He looked up at Glitter, and for an instant, when their eyes met, Glitter could've sworn she saw a flash of silver.

CRIMSON NOON

First published in *Blood in the Soil, Terror on the Wind,*
edited by Kenneth W. Cain (Brigid's Gate Press)

The convoy of wagons crawled through the desert like an orderly line of ants. From his vantage point atop a rocky outcrop, the midday sun beating down on his uncovered head, Boy reached for his canteen, unstoppered it, and took a swig of warm water, all without ever taking his eyes off the wagons. He hadn't seen newcomers arrive in Mirage for a long while. Not since most of the gold prospectors had headed elsewhere in search of better mines and richer seams.

"Boy!"

Old Man Norris could holler louder than anyone else in Mirage, even above the noise of the miners talking and laughing as they ate lunch. Boy leaped to his feet and scrambled down the dusty cliff-side, then sprinted towards the mine entrance as fast as his legs could carry him.

"Boy!"

By the time he reached the mine shaft, Boy was panting, and Old Man Norris was red-faced and furious. He thwacked Boy on the side of the head, leaving his left ear stinging.

"What do you think you're doing, boy, idling when there's work to be done?"

"I seen a convoy," Boy said, pointing.

"And I've seen a pile of ore needs washing, so get to it!" Norris shoved Boy hard in the direction of the river, and Boy lost his footing, muttering under his breath as he stumbled and almost fell.

"You got something to say, boy?" Norris snapped.

Boy's face burned. He looked back over his shoulder, but refused to meet Norris's eye. "No."

"No, *sir.*"

"No, sir."

"Better. Get that pile sorted by nightfall, or there'll be no supper for you."

Boy stared at a point somewhere to the left of Norris's head. "Yes, sir."

✷∵✦∵✦∵✦∵✦∵✦∵

As evening fell, Boy walked back to the town, chewing on the hunk of bread Norris had given him for supper. The convoy of wagons was parked at the far end of Mirage's main street. Mirage's only street, in fact. With the arrival of the newcomers in their wagons, the population of Mirage might as well have doubled.

Main Street was almost as busy as Boy remembered it being when he was small, back when the mine was new and the seams still rich with gold. There were four wagons, several horses, and more people than he could count. He'd heard there were other towns far bigger than Mirage—cities, even, with many streets and hundreds of people, and he wondered whether the convoy had come from one of those places.

He loitered in the shadow of the saloon where Miss Estrella worked and watched the strangers settle around their campfire, laughing and talking. Some of the younger men tied up their horses and swaggered into the saloon. Boy narrowed his eyes as they passed, and once their backs were turned, he cocked two fingers at them like a pistol and pretended to fire.

The women of the convoy set up a cooking pot above the fire, and before long the air filled with the scent of sizzling meat. Boy's stomach rumbled. Light poured from the saloon windows, and the sound of laughter rang out from within. Some nights, Miss Estrella would try to sneak him extra food from the saloon's kitchen. But tonight, Boy doubted she'd have the time to take notice of him.

Instead, he drifted closer to the warmth of the fire and the smell of cooking—not hoping for anything, really, but drawn all the same. The women, busy with their tasks and the children scurrying around their feet, paid no attention to him. The older men—the ones who hadn't gone to the saloon—gave him a quick look up and down and turned back to their bowls of stew.

The only person whose eyes lingered on him was a small, pale girl with lank blonde hair and a gaunt face. Boy guessed she was probably around his age, or a little older, perhaps. As one of the women ladled stew into her bowl, the girl gazed at him across the fire, not with interest or curiosity, just a blank, distant stare. Once her bowl was full, she stood and, with a nod towards Boy, slipped behind one of the wagons.

Boy checked no one else was watching and followed her. She was waiting, and she held the bowl out to him with both hands.

"Take it," she said. "You look like you need it." There was an unfamiliar lilt to her accent that Boy couldn't quite place. It reminded him of a Polish man who'd visited the town once.

"What about you?" he asked.

The girl shrugged. Her dress hung loosely off her bones. "I'm not hungry."

Boy hesitated. She sure *looked* hungry. Starving, in fact. She was so thin it made him wince. But her people had a big pot full stew. If she wanted more, she could get more. And the thought of trying to sleep with just a hunk of bread to fill his belly made him want to cry. He took the bowl and sat behind the wagon to guzzle down the stew, savoring every chunk of meat. When he was done, he looked around for the girl, but she was gone.

::*:*:*:*:*:*:

At noon the next day, Boy was sifting ore by the river when he heard screaming. He dropped his sieve and ran to the mine entrance, clambering on top of a discarded cart to see over the heads of the gathered crowd. There, amid the clamor, stood Larry Ketch, shivering and convulsing in the bright sun, howling as though the light itself burned him. Ketch raised his hands to his face; they were covered in sores, blistering even as he stood there, breaking and splitting into bloody gashes that tore down his arms, up his chest, across his face—everywhere the light touched. He screamed and whirled around mindlessly, falling on the nearest miner, knocking the big man to the ground as though he were no more than a feather.

The big miner—Crawford, his name was—tried to fight off his attacker to no avail. Ketch was like a rabid animal, bleeding and screaming and now puking blood all over Crawford's face. Crawford roared and threw him aside, but Ketch leaped onto him again, sinking his teeth straight into Crawford's throat. There was a hideous *rip* of flesh, and Ketch drew back, blood and gristle hanging from between his teeth. He turned to look directly at Boy, who froze, too terrified to move or even breathe. Ketch's eyes were wild. Glazed. There was nothing human left in them at all. Just hunger. Crawford let out a strangled groan, blood bubbling from the gash in his throat.

For a moment, Boy was certain he would be next. Then shots rang out. Ketch shuddered and slumped forward, a dead weight on top of Crawford's chest.

The other miners rushed to help him, dragging Ketch's body away, surrounding Crawford as they tried to stem the bleeding from his throat. Their backs formed an impassible wall, and even from his cart, Boy couldn't see anything anymore. Quietly, unnoticed, he climbed down and ran all the way back to town.

✶✦✶✦✶✦✶✦✶

That night, after Crawford had been taken home to recover from his wounds, Sheriff O'Connell called a town meeting in the saloon. None of the newcomers were invited. Neither was Boy. He loitered outside the bar's back door until Estrella came out, wiping her hands on her apron. People said Estrella's mother had been Spanish, which might've explained her golden-brown skin and dark eyes. For as long as he could remember, Boy had thought of her as the most beautiful woman he'd ever seen. If he'd had a mother, he thought, she might've looked like that.

"Don't you have a bed to go to?" Estrella asked.

Boy shrugged. He usually slept in the loft above the stables, where it was warm and dry, and the stray dogs kept him company. Sometimes if it was hot, he slept under the stars and imagined he was a bounty hunter camping out as he tracked his prey.

He stared at Estrella until she sighed and let him into the kitchen.

"You saw what happened at the mineshaft?" she asked, cutting a hunk of bread and handing it to him.

Boy nodded. "Yes, ma'am."

"People are saying ..." Estrella glanced over her

shoulder to make sure there was nobody else in the kitchen and lowered her voice. "They're saying Ketch attacked Crawford. Like he was trying to … to eat him."

Boy looked down at his bread and nodded again. Truth be told, he'd been off his feed all day after watching that happen.

"You must've been so scared." Estrella put an arm around his shoulders and led him to a seat near the stove.

"No, ma'am." Boy lifted his chin. "Not scared."

Estrella smiled. She had a sweet smile. Boy liked the way her cheeks dimpled.

"No, of course not. A future gunslinger like yourself would never be scared. But me? I'm frightened. So if you wanted to sleep here in the kitchen tonight, you know, just so I know you're here to take care of me … I wouldn't tell anybody, you understand?"

"I can do that, ma'am," Boy said. "If it makes you feel better."

Estrella brushed the top of his head with her palm as she headed back out to the bar. "Thank you, kind sir. It does."

✶∴✦∴✦∴✦∴✶

When Estrella went back out to the bar, Boy followed her to the door and peered through the crack into the warm glow of the saloon. Sheriff O'Connell held court from his favorite table facing the door, while Mirage's townsfolk gathered in a semicircle around him. He told them he was ordering a halt to activities at the mine until such time as the cause of Ketch's 'sickness' could be found out.

"It's got something to do with those new folk," one of the miners called out. "Weren't no problems in this town before they showed up here."

Several others nodded their agreement, but O'Connell shook his head. "We don't know that. None of them have even been near the mine, to my knowledge."

"To *your* knowledge," Norris parroted back. "And what do you think they're here for in the first place?"

"Pull in your horns," said O'Connell. "They're from New York City. On their way to one of the new mines on the West Coast."

"Sure, that's what they told you. Funny they should show up just a few weeks after we found a new untapped seam, though, ain't it? You oughta go down there and tell them to move on, see how they take it."

"Quit your whining, Norris," Estrella said. "They're good for business."

Norris snorted. "Good for *your* business, maybe. We can't all work on our backs."

Boy wasn't sure how Estrella made her money, but

hearing Norris say that sent a rush of hot blood to his cheeks, nonetheless. He turned back to the dark kitchen and lay down on the rug in front of the flickering embers of the fire.

Boy slept badly. Ketch's face kept intruding into his dreams, and he woke in a cold sweat, thinking of the man's crazed, hungry eyes. With the mine closed there was nothing for Boy to do to earn his bread that day, and he decided to head up to the strangers' encampment, hoping he could persuade the pale girl to give him a little more food. He circled the wagons a few times, but there was no sign of her anywhere, and eventually one of the gruff old men chased him off. Instead, Boy sauntered down Main Street, peering in the windows of the grocer's and the tobacconist's to see what everybody was up to. When he reached the blacksmith's, he was amazed to see Crawford on his way out. He had a rag wrapped around his throat, but otherwise there was no hint of what Ketch had done to him the day before.

"What's the matter with you, boy? You look nervous as a cat in a room full o' rockers." He patted Boy on the shoulder, then stopped. Froze. Looked up at the sun blazing a hole in the cloudless blue sky. Boy had only a split second to realize something was wrong before Crawford's mouth opened in a silent scream. His skin began to boil and split, just as Ketch's had the day before.

Boy didn't wait around to see what happened next. He turned tail and fled to the stables, where he burst through the door and scrambled up the ladder to the hayloft. From the loft's tiny window, he peered out at Crawford shrieking and howling and vomiting blood. The Sheriff and some of the storekeepers ran out to see what the matter was, and one of them, Boy couldn't quite see which, put a bullet in Crawford's chest. Crawford hit the dirt, and Boy was sure he was dead, but then he flipped over and crawled towards the Sheriff, dragging himself along with his fingers. His mouth opened wide. His eyes were ... they were *bleeding.*

The Sheriff took aim, but before he could shoot, Crawford clamped his jaws around O'Connell's ankle. O'Connell fired wildly, and so did the others, letting off their pistols until Crawford finally went limp, face down in the dust.

Boy turned and flung himself back against the wall, chest heaving with his sharp breaths. He was shaking all over. Estrella was right. He *was* scared. Scared of where this sickness was coming from. Scared of who might be next. Of the thought that it might be *him.*

⋅⋅*⋅*⋅*⋅*

Boy stayed in the loft until nightfall, when he slipped out onto Main Street. The darkness covered him like a cloak, making him feel safer. He crept to the saloon, backing hurriedly away from the front door as a group of men from the wagon camp headed inside. Then, gathering his courage and hoping he would not be spotted, he sneaked in after them.

The saloon was filled with light and music, busier than Boy had ever seen it before. Sheriff O'Connell sat at the bar, knocking back a whiskey, his leg wrapped in bandages and propped on the stool next to him. The others were giving him a wide berth, but the Sheriff seemed too preoccupied with his drink to care. Boy stared for a long moment, half expecting him to start bleeding and growling right before his eyes, but nothing happened.

"It's them, I'm telling you," somebody snarled, glaring across at the newcomers who'd just entered the bar. "They've brought something evil with them. Weren't no problems in Mirage before *they* showed up."

"There were plenty o' problems in Mirage before they showed up," O'Connell replied. "I don't want no trouble tonight."

But Boy could tell from the look on the men's' faces that there was trouble brewing, anyhow. He hung around until

Estrella came out to the bar and mouthed at him to get gone. Then he slipped back out into the dark night and headed for the camp. Perhaps the pale girl would have some food for him. Perhaps she might even *know* something. He didn't like the thought of Estrella in there, standing right by O'Connell as he drank. If the men were right, and the sickness had something to do with the newcomers, perhaps the pale girl could tell him how they were spreading it. Maybe even how to stop it. Boy imagined himself rushing back to the saloon, being the one to save Estrella just in time. The thought made him puff out his chest a little as he reached the camp.

This time, the pale girl was there, sitting in front of the campfire, gazing into the flames. When Boy caught her eye, he put his finger to his lips and beckoned to her. Then he headed behind one of the wagons and waited.

For a moment he thought she wouldn't come, but eventually he heard the soft pad of her feet, and she rounded the corner. She looked better than she had the last time he'd seen her. Her face was rounder, her lips more red. He thought she might even be approaching Estrella, in terms of prettiness.

"I don't have any stew tonight," she whispered. "You're too late."

"I don't need no stew," Boy replied. "You gotta tell me

what's going on."

"What?"

"The blood sickness. Your family brought it here. That's what everyone's saying."

"I don't know anything about that," the girl said. "Besides, they're not my family."

"They're not?"

She shook her head, biting her lip. "I don't have any family. They're just … I had to get out of New York, and they let me hitch a ride, that's all."

Boy shrugged. "Doesn't matter what they are. There's gonna be trouble if they don't get gone soon. And you with 'em."

"Why?"

"Why what?"

"Why'd you care? You don't know me."

"You were kind to me, is all."

The girl approached him. She placed a gentle hand on his arm, and all the hairs on Boy's skin stood up. "I can't make them leave," she said. "They won't listen to me."

Boy thought of Estrella. "Then you've gotta tell me how to stop the sickness," he said.

"You can't stop it. Just … please do me a favor?"

"What's that?"

The girl leaned in close, gripping his arm. "Promise me

you won't come here during the day."

Shouts rang out across the camp. Boy ran to look out from behind the wagon. Men were fighting outside the saloon—the newcomers against the townsfolk, the women and children crowding around to watch, to goad them on or beg them to stop. Then Sheriff O'Connell limped out and fired three shots into the sky.

"Get back to your homes," he growled. "Or I'll be putting bullets in the lot of you."

The men grumbled, and some of them swore or spat at one another, but the people of Mirage respected O'Connell enough to let the argument go—for now. Boy turned back to the girl, meaning to ask for her name, but she was gone.

★ ∴ ★ ∴ ★ ∴ ★

Morning came, and Boy stirred in his bed of hay, thinking on the girl's words. *Promise me you won't come here during the day.* It seemed to Boy that the lesions on Ketch and Crawford's skin had only appeared when they stepped into the midday sun. Did the girl know something after all? She'd said she didn't, but could he really trust a newcomer?

Boy crept out from his loft and watched the people of Mirage prepare for Ketch and Crawford's funeral. They were fearful enough of the sickness to want to burn the bodies and were building a pyre several feet high at the far end of Main Street, where the wind would blow the smoke away from the town. Boy sat on the steps of the General Store and counted the minutes as the sun crawled higher and higher in the sky. The back of his neck prickled with sweat. As noon approached, he realized he was holding his breath.

The townsfolk lit the pyre, the flames quickly flaring into a blaze. Sheriff O'Connell limped down the center of Main Street at the head of the funeral procession. Behind him was Old Man Norris and the rest of the miners, as well as Estrella and the other girls from the saloon, veiled in black. O'Connell stopped in front of the bonfire, turning his face to the sky. Boy put his hands over his eyes, peeking out from between his fingers.

And then it happened.

Not just the Sheriff, but some of the miners, too. Even some of the girls from the saloon. All of them clutched at their faces as the lesions took hold. They screamed, they howled, they shuddered and fell on each other, foaming at the mouths, bleeding at the eyes. Boy took flight and ran, fast as he could, around the back of the General Store, behind the buildings on Main Street, until he reached the wagon camp.

He burst into the middle of the camp, disturbing women with their laundry hanging out by the fire, men cleaning their guns, children kicking around a stray clump of tumble-weed.

"Help!" he shouted. "Help, please! You've got to help us!"

The strangers didn't have to ask what the matter was. The shouting from Main Street was enough to alert them. The men called instructions to each other, loaded their guns up, mobilizing with a weary resignation, as though they'd dealt with something like this before. Boy followed them back to town, thinking of Estrella. He wished he had a gun. He wished he wasn't so scared.

When they reached Main Street, they found a bloodbath. The folk afflicted with the sickness had turned on the others, and now the whole town was feral. Bodies crawled over one another. Faces that had once been human leered with red, dripping teeth. Black blood soaked into the dust.

The strangers released shot after shot, and Boy, hiding behind their legs and shaking so hard he could barely stand, watched the townsfolk fall. Sheriff O'Connell. Old Man Norris. The miners and the grocer and the girls from the saloon. The only people he'd known in his short life. The air was sharp with the metallic scent of blood. Boy didn't want to look, but he had to. He had to know if Estrella was still alive.

And then he saw her. Peering out from behind the saloon

door. She spotted him and waved him over, and he ran as fast as he could, slamming into her, burying his face in her stomach. To his intense shame, he started to cry, and then he couldn't stop. The tears came in great, gulping waves that wracked his whole body. He didn't want Estrella to see him like this, but at the same time, he didn't care. He just wanted to escape. To be somewhere—anywhere—else.

"Come on." Estrella pulled him into the saloon, leading him through the bar and out of the door at the back of the kitchen. Together they sneaked into the stables, and Estrella freed one of the horses. It was spooked by the noise of the shooting, and it took a lot of coaxing to get it out the door, but soon they were riding away from town. Boy sat between Estrella's legs, clinging desperately to the horse's mane while the saloon girl held him by the waist.

"Wait!" he cried, as they passed the wagon camp. "The girl!"

Estrella slowed the horse. "What girl?"

Boy was already wriggling his way out of her grip, slipping off the horse's back. "I can't go without her."

He dropped to the ground and ran over to the wagons, ignoring the stares of the women and children still huddled there.

"Girl!" he shouted. "Pale girl! Where are you?"

"Get out of here, you little fool," one of the women

yelled. "They'll be back soon. Just go!"

Boy span to face her. "Where is she? The pale girl?"

The woman's face hardened. She pointed to one of the wagons. "You want to take her, be our guest. Just don't say we didn't warn you."

Boy sped past her and clambered into the wagon. It was dark and musty and filled with furniture. It took his eyes a moment to adjust, and at first he stumbled around blindly. Eventually, he spotted the girl, crouched in the darkest corner. No, not just crouched. Locked up in a cage. Anger boiled in Boy's stomach. How could her people do this to her?

As he approached, she shook her head hurriedly, trying to wave him away.

"Don't," she whispered. "Don't."

"Don't worry." Boy searched for something that would break the lock. "I'm going to get you out of here."

Her pale eyes followed him around the room. "Don't."

Boy opened a cabinet and rooted around until he found something that felt heavy in his hand. A brass ornament of some sort. Approaching the cage, he slammed it against the lock as hard as he could, until it broke and the door swung open. He grabbed the girl's arm and tugged at her, but she stayed stubbornly in place. A faint shaft of sunlight coming from the entrance to the wagon grazed her face, and in the glow she looked prettier than ever, her lips and cheeks now rosy red.

"Come on!" he hissed. "Please."

"I can't." She was shaking. "I can't go out there."

"It's all right. We've got a horse. We can ride to the next town. We'll be safe there. Please."

The girl stared at him, her breath coming fast and shallow. There was a strange look in her eyes. She licked her lips.

"Come on," he tried again.

Slowly, her eyes never leaving his face, the girl crept out of her cage. The moment she was free, Boy pulled her out of the wagon and the two of them hopped down to the ground. The women and children watched as they ran across the camp to where Estrella waited with the horse, but nobody tried to stop them.

"Quickly, quickly!" Estrella looked over her shoulder at the town. The funeral pyre must have spread; smoke rose high into the air, almost blotting out the sun. Shadowy figures approached the camp—the men returning with their guns.

Estrella pulled the children up onto the horse in front of her, then spurred it on, picking up speed across the empty desert. The girl grasped the horse's mane, and Boy clung to her, burying his face in her hair. She smelled strange.

Almost of … burning.

"Don't worry," he told her. "We'll be safe soon. Why were they keeping you in there?"

"I told you!" the girl said, her voice a choked sob. "I told you … not to come … in the daylight."

She twisted round, her face filling Boy's vision. Her eyes blazed red and her mouth opened wide, displaying teeth sharp as nails. Hissing, she threw herself at him, and he hit the ground with a thud that jarred all the air from his lungs. And then she was on him, pinning him down with her hands on his shoulders, drooling blood onto his face. Boy kicked his heels against the ground, trying to push himself back. Trying to get out from under her grip. It was impossible. Where was Estrella? Had she fallen from the horse? Was she hurt?

He couldn't tell. There was nothing now—nothing but the girl's snarling face, looming in, aiming for his throat. It was her, had been her all along. She had brought the sickness to Mirage. But somewhere in her eyes, behind the hunger and the animal fury, he saw something else—fear. The eyes of a girl who knew what she was. Knew what she was doing. Who had tried to warn him. And then her teeth sank into his flesh, and all went dark.

It was almost midnight in the town of Red Creek when a local drunk emerged from the saloon and spotted a lone horse winding its way into town. He peered at it, trying to make sense of the dark shape through his blurred vision. The horse stopped, and someone dropped from its back. A woman, and two children with her.

One hand on his pistol, the drunk staggered over to meet the newcomer. Her face was gaunt and wan in the moonlight. Hungry. The children seemed drowsy, as though they'd been sleeping. One was a pale girl with hair almost as silver as the moon, the other a skinny little urchin boy.

"Spare a bed for the night, sir?" the woman asked. She was pretty—beautiful, even—and the drunk could hardly believe his luck. He glanced around to make sure that nobody else had noticed them, but the streets of Red Creek were silent.

"Y'all look like you could use a decent meal," he slurred, his eyes lingering on the boy, who was the most starved looking of them all. But to his surprise, the boy shook his head.

"No thank you, sir," Boy said, his lips curling into a smile. "We can wait until morning."

Spellbound

First published in *SLASH-HER*,
edited by Janine Pipe (Kandisha Press)

Fliss spins the empty cola bottle with a flick of her wrist, and I watch it wobble to a halt amongst the detritus of burger wrappers. *Please, don't let it land on me.*

It does.

"Truth or dare?" Fliss shouts over the cacophony of the nearby slot machines. The mall's about to close, but the arcade games are still blaring away to themselves: lights flashing, demo music playing.

"Truth," I reply, and immediately regret it. I can feel the other girls watching me, but I look only at Fliss. Over her left shoulder, gold letters spell out the word 'JACKPOT' against a black screen. They flash a few times, then fade away in a shower of sparks. Jackpot, indeed. This is the moment Fliss has been waiting for. I know exactly what she's going to ask.

"Have you ever …" a sly smile creeps across her face, "had a near-death experience?"

That … wasn't what I was expecting. I'd steeled myself for what I thought was the inevitable question about Dylan Chalmers: *How did you convince him to want you back? Tell the truth: you used the love spell, didn't you?* I don't know how to respond to this.

I take a swig of my cola and look Fliss in the eyes. Those pretty blue eyes beneath a heavy blonde fringe. The eyes that persuaded Dylan to cheat on me over the summer. It's nearly Halloween now and she's never let me forget it. And now, just to add insult to injury, those eyes flick briefly towards my wrists and I realize that she *knows*.

Well, fuck her.

"I changed my mind," I say. "Dare."

Fliss snorts. "You can't change your mind, Ally."

She glances at the rest of the coven for support. Redheaded Maddie averts her eyes, staying out of it. Jazz shrugs and lights a cigarette, in clear defiance of the no-smoking sign above her head. Only Rhona looks like she might speak up, and it's a fifty-fifty chance whether she'll side with me or Fliss. She frowns, weighing us up. I clench my fingers around the neck of my bottle and try not to draw attention to the bracelets around my wrists, hiding the scars. If Rhona gets a whiff that there might be a juicy story to be told, she's not going to let up until she hears it.

Luckily for me, the idea of a dare seems to appeal to Rhona, and she says, "Let her change her mind, Fliss. This place is about to close, anyway. We need something else to do."

Fliss slumps back in her chair and folds her arms, looking sullen. Nobody argues with Rhona.

"You think of a dare, then," Fliss says.

"All right."

Rhona's gaze strays to the other side of the food court, where the last few stragglers are leaving the mall's indoor theme park. Little kids hyped up on candy and soda, their harassed-looking parents in tow. Behind them, an employee in a leprechaun costume locks the gates to Shamrock Fair and walks away toward the multi-story car park.

"I dare you to break into Shamrock Fair."

"Fuck off," I say.

But Dylan and I used to sneak in there after his shifts running the Rainbow Coaster, and the rest of the coven know it. As long as the owners haven't changed the security code on the employee entrance, we can get in, easy. Knowing their lax attitude to security, I'm betting they haven't.

"Come on, Ally," Jazz says. "Your choice. Get us into Shamrock Fair, or answer the question."

There's no way I'm answering Fliss's question, so I guess I'm doing this.

"Fine." I down the last of my drink and stand up. "We'd better be quick."

＊ ＊ ＊ ＊ ＊ ＊ ＊ ＊ ＊ ＊

We hunker down behind a bank of bins at the edge of the food court until the lights snap off and the slot machines power down for the night. Then, once we're sure everybody else has gone, the five of us creep out and hurry towards the employee entrance between Chicken Hut and Kwik Burger.

"If someone catches us, we're going to get done for trespassing," Maddie whispers, hanging back.

"Don't be stupid." Jazz grabs her arm and drags her along. "Look, the place is deserted."

The other girls cluster around me, keeping watch while I approach the keypad. I punch in the code and wait, holding my breath. There's a flutter of excitement inside my chest, and it surprises me. It's the first actual feeling I've felt in a while. Definitely the first since I left hospital. But then I think of the times I had with Dylan, sneaking in here, riding the Rainbow Coaster all by ourselves, kissing in the ball pit in Leprechaun's Castle, and the old gaping hole of despair opens in my stomach again.

The door clicks open and I usher the others inside, letting it slam behind us. We run, giggling, down the corridor, and burst out beneath the vast glass roof of the theme park.

Above us, the multi-colored track of the Rainbow Coaster snakes close to the starless sky, then drops sharply, dipping near to the ground at points. Beneath it are smaller rides—the pirate ship, the carousel, the lazy river with the swan boats leashed to the dock. And, the backdrop to it all, the giant Leprechaun's Castle soft play, complete with spiral sides and a hall of mirrors. It was the scene of many a happy childhood birthday party for all of us, back before we were witches. Before all the useless spells and backstabbing and cheating came between us. Suddenly, being here seems like fate. I'm getting swept up in the moment—I'm almost giddy with it. This is my opportunity to erase the memory of all those nights with Dylan, the cheating asshole, and replace them with something else.

I grin.

"What shall we go on first?"

✶⋆✶⋆✶⋆✶

We run for the Rainbow Coaster, pelting along the dimly lit

'street' with its fake cobbles, shrieking and laughing. It's only when we get there that I realize one of us is missing.

"Jazz?"

No answer. I scan the street, but there's no sign of her.

"Jazz, stop fucking about," Rhona chimes in. "Hurry up! We're going on the coaster, with or without you."

Still nothing.

"Perhaps she went to raid the candy store," I say.

"Fuck her." Fliss hops over the barrier and into the front carriage. "Start it up, Maddie."

"Why me?" Maddie says.

"Because you're fucking scared of rollercoasters, that's why." Rhona rolls her eyes and drops into the carriage next to Fliss. I give Maddie an apologetic shrug and take a seat just behind them. Maddie, looking sulky, disappears into the operator's cabin.

A moment later, the coaster shudders to life. We pull the barriers down across our knees as lights illuminate along the track, and the train begins to move.

"Jazz, you're missing out!" Fliss screams when we hit the first drop. And then we're zooming around, yelling at the top of our lungs. Laughing. Happy.

Until we see it.

At first, it's not much more than a shadow in the semi-darkness. A silhouetted figure hanging beneath the highest point of the track ahead, tied up by its wrists. Some kind of prop I hadn't noticed before? Just another of the plastic leprechauns that litter the fair? Weird place to put it. Plus, I'm sure I didn't notice it on our first few circuits of the track.

It's only when we get up close that I realize what it actually is. Not a plastic leprechaun. Not at all.

It's Jazz.

"Stop! Stop the coaster!"

But even as I'm shouting, knowing Maddie's too far away to hear, the coaster's already rolling over the track above Jazz, wheels slicing through the ropes. I look over my shoulder just in time to see her fall, but then we whip around a corner and she's out of sight.

"Jazz!"

"Maddie!"

We're all screaming now, waving our arms, trying to get Maddie to stop the ride. She must've heard us, because once we get back to the operator's cabin, the coaster rolls to a halt. We scramble out.

"Was that really Jazz?" Rhona asks. "How did she get up there?" Her voice is shaking—that's not like Rhona at all.

"We've got to find her. Maddie, come on." I look at the operator's cabin. It's empty. "Where's Maddie?"

"Never mind her." Fliss tugs my arm. "Let's get to Jazz."

We pelt down the main street, over the miniature train track and past the candy-floss stand, until we reach Jazz. Her legs are broken, and she's lying all mangled and twisted, but it wasn't the fall that killed her. It's the way she's been slashed right down the middle, from neck to guts, so that her entrails spill out all over the cobbles.

The person who did this can't be far away. I start hyper-ventilating. I'm sure I'm going to be sick. And then I am. Throwing up into the gaping mouth of a leprechaun-themed trash can.

"Who did this?" Rhona says over the sounds of my retching.

"Who the hell cares?" Fliss replies. "We have to get the fuck out of here!"

There's no arguing with that. I lift my head and wipe my mouth with the back of my hand, trying to ignore both the roiling of my stomach and the misshapen mass of flesh that used to be Jazz. On trembling legs, I follow the others back to the employee's entrance. It's only when the door is in sight that I remember we've left someone behind.

"Wait!" I cry. "What about Maddie?"

"Maddie can take care of herself." Rhona looks back at me. "I'm not risking running into whoever did that to Jazz."

I'm shaking, and I feel faint, but one thing's clear in my mind: "I'm not leaving Maddie here on her own."

Trying to look braver than I feel, I stride back the way we came, shouting for Maddie. A moment later, Fliss is at my side.

"We should stick together," she says. "And besides …" I follow her gaze as she glances back to where Rhona's banging on the door, "we're locked in here."

Shit.

My stomach flips again.

"Maddie!" I shout. "Maddie!"

An ear-piercing screech rings across the theme park. I slam my hands over my ears. Feedback. There's an observation desk high above the Leprechaun's Castle, where an employee usually sits to monitor the rides and make announcements over the intercom. With a crackle, the speaker comes to life.

"Welcome to Murderland!"

The voice is vaguely male, high-pitched, distorted.

"Are you looking for my pot of gold, ladies? You'll find it … at the end of the rainbow!"

The voice cackles, and feedback splits the air again before the intercom flicks off. I look at Fliss, then Rhona, who's hurrying to catch up.

"Who the fuck are you, you sicko?" Rhona screams at the glass roof.

"A pot of gold at the end of the rainbow?" I say. "Do you

think he means Maddie?"

"I think it's time we called the cops." Fliss pulls out her mobile.

"No signal inside Shamrock Fair," I remind her.

She stares at her phone. "Shit. You're right."

"The end of the rainbow," Rhona muses. "The Rainbow Coaster. You don't think …?"

I'm already moving. Because it's occurred to me: the Rainbow Coaster ends at the operator's cabin. We didn't see Maddie there, but we just assumed she would be standing up, visible through the window. What if she was there all along? I break into a run, take the stairs to the cabin two at a time. Fling open the door.

And there she is. Slumped on the floor, cut from neck to navel, just like Jazz was. And out of her spills …

"What the hell *is* that?" Rhona asks.

I pluck one of the gold plastic coins between my fingers. It's covered in blood.

"Leprechaun's Gold," I say, turning it to show her.

They're the tokens you use to pay for the rides. The sicko has stuffed Maddie full of them, and now they're spilling out along with her guts.

"Why is this happening to us?!" Fliss sounds hysterical. I would be too, if I hadn't gone completely numb. I go to her, try to put my arms around her, but she pushes me away, her eyes streaming with tears.

"Why are you doing this?" I scream, facing the observation deck. "We haven't done anything to you!"

The ear-piercing screech returns, along with the cold, high-pitched cackle.

"Oh, but you did," echoes the voice. *"You did something ... unforgivable. Now. Who wants to be next? Eenie, meenie, miney ..."*

"I'm not listening to any more of this," Rhona says. "We've got to find another way out of here."

A host of possibilities fill my mind. All the kids at school we sold our 'spells' to. The bottles of love potion that were really just water and food coloring. The lists of meaningless instructions involving pentacles and candles. Could our tormentor be a disappointed customer?

What does it matter? I try to focus. There has to be another way out. The front gates are locked. The employee entrance is locked. But Dylan knew this place like the back of his hand, and I'm sure he took me out another way once.

"At the back of Leprechaun's Palace," I hiss, not knowing whether the killer can overhear us. "There's a fire exit that leads out of the hall of mirrors."

"Then what are we waiting for?" Rhona strides off, but I grab her arm.

"Wait," I say, reaching for Fliss with my other hand.

189

"We stay together. Keep each other in sight at all times. He's picking us off one by one. We can't let that happen."

"Damn, Ally. Who made you survival expert all of a sudden?" Fliss says, her gaze drifting to my wrists. *Survival expert.* Yeah, I guess it does sound ironic, under the circumstances. Perhaps this killer is only here to give me what I wanted, after all.

The truth is, I wanted to die. That's the secret Fliss got wind of, somehow. I made my parents keep it a secret, and I sure as hell never told anyone else, so how did Fliss, of all people, find out? She was the last person in the world I wanted to know. My ex-best friend who stole my boyfriend.

But as we creep into the foyer of Leprechaun's Palace, passing the ball pit at the bottom of the spiral slide, I cling to her hand and feel a sudden surge of tenderness for her. This is *Fliss*, after all. The girl who sat next to me on my first day in class, aged six, when I'd just moved into town. The girl who brought me here, to Shamrock Fair, for the first time, on her eighth birthday. The girl who started our 'coven', never mind that it was all bullshit. I squeeze her fingers.

"We're going to get out of here," I tell her. "It's going to be okay."

We enter the hall of mirrors, and our distorted reflections loom from all angles. The glass walls close in on me. It's tight and claustrophobic, and I can't remember how to find the fire escape. I lead the others around for what feels like hours, heart thudding, palms sweating, convinced they're following me into certain death. And then—thank God!—I see it. A nondescript door at the end of a glass corridor, designed to look like a dead end. I drop the other girls' hands and run to open it, pushing down on the lever.

It doesn't budge.

Shit.

Shit, shit, shit.

I go on pushing, banging on the door with my fists. Eventually, defeated, I turn to find Fliss close behind me, looking equally panicked. But Rhona …

"Rhona!"

She's gone. Rhona is nowhere to be seen. How did we lose her? Only a moment ago, I was holding her hand. But I let go, and now she's gone. I grab Fliss's hand. Cling to it again. There's no way I'm letting her go, too. Her blue eyes bore into mine, almost shining in the dim light.

"Where did she go?" I whisper.

The intercom crackles again. Of course: from the observation deck, the killer can see down into the glass maze. He can see everything. He watched us walk right in here—right into a trap.

"Rhona won't be joining you, I'm afraid."

It's that laugh again, rising into a squeal. It makes my blood freeze. Where have I heard that laugh before?

As if on cue, the voice speaks again. *"C'mere and kiss me lucky shamrock, girls!"*

Dylan.

It couldn't be ... could it? But that's his ridiculous leprechaun routine he used to do when he was in costume. The laugh was part of it. I can't believe I didn't recognize it right away. I suppose because the idea that Dylan would do this to me and my friends is just ... unthinkable.

I look at Fliss, and I can see she's had the same realization. We make a silent agreement not to waste time discussing it.

"Let's get out of this maze," she whispers, and I nod.

Together, holding hands, we retrace our steps out of the hall of mirrors. A left turn here, a right turn there, another left and ... The door. We're back where we started. The laugh crackles over the intercom.

"Keep trying, ladies!"

"What's wrong with you?!" I shout. "What have you done with Rhona?"

No answer. We keep walking, round and round and round. I imagine Rhona lying somewhere, disemboweled like the others, Leprechaun's Gold spewing from her insides, and I want to cry. Any moment, Dylan could spring on us and we'll suffer the same fate. Dylan, for God's sake. *Dylan.* My boyfriend. The guy I slit my wrists for. How could he do this to us?

It wasn't really about Dylan, though, the wrist-cutting. Not really. It was about Fliss. A boyfriend is one thing, a best friend is another. The thing that destroyed me—the thing that really ate me up inside until I didn't want to live anymore—was the thought that my best friend could lie to me, go behind my back like that. All those years of best friendship, thrown away in one night. Fliss, with her pretty fucking blue eyes and her pretty fucking blonde hair. She was convinced I'd used the love spell on Dylan. For some reason, she thought I'd got it to work and was holding out on her, all because she couldn't believe Dylan would ever really like *me.* I hated her. I still hate her. And now I'm stuck with her, in this maze, and we're going to die together.

It's exactly what I've been fantasizing about for weeks. It's almost as though I brought this upon us. Dylan is doing me a favor. At least if I go down this time I'll take her with me.

Have you ever had a near-death experience?

Fucking bitch.

"Ally!" Fliss tries to yank her hand from my grip. "Let go, you're hurting me!"

Before I can respond, we turn a corner and step out of

the maze. Ahead of us is the ball pit at the bottom of the spiral slide. To the left, a set of stairs, roped off, hung with a "Staff Only" sign.

"The observation deck," I whisper to Fliss. "We can get up there. Take him by surprise."

We're halfway to the stairs when we see Rhona come sliding down the spiral slide and crash into the ball pit, leaving a bloody smear behind her. I rush over as she disappears beneath the rainbow of balls, and it's only then I realize I've let go of Fliss's hand again. For a moment I hesitate, torn between looking behind me to check that Fliss is still there, and diving into the ball pit to search for Rhona. For all I know, Rhona might still be alive. But Fliss—

I turn around.

Fliss is gone.

I plunge into the ball pool and pull Rhona out. Her head is all but severed from her neck, and when I try to pick her up it flops back, exposing a gory mess of blood and vertebrae. I drop her and slump against the wall of the ball pit, crying, cursing myself. Rhona is dead. Maddie is dead. Jazz is dead. And my moment of hesitation might have cost Fliss her life, too. Why didn't Dylan just come for me? Surely it's me he wants, and I don't give a shit if he kills me, anyway. I was the one who wanted to die, not Fliss. This isn't fair.

Except I don't. I don't want to die. Maybe it's the

adrenaline surging through my veins, but when I hear the creak of a footstep on the stairs behind me, I'm overcome with the need to *live*. All at once, my future flashes before my eyes. College. My wedding. Children. All the things that Rhona and Maddie and Jazz won't get to experience. And for what? Because I wouldn't go back to Dylan after he cheated on me?

Clenching my fists, I turn to face him.

Except it's not him coming down the stairs. It's Fliss, clutching a bloody knife.

"Did you get him?" I ask, my voice hushed, glancing up at the observation deck.

"I got him." Fliss is breathing fast, her cheeks flushed. "Come and see."

I follow her upstairs. There, lying on the floor next to a worn desk chair, is Dylan, still in his leprechaun costume, his green jacket stained with blood. Above him is the control panel with its intercom system and CCTV screens showing the bodies of Rhona, Maddie, and Jazz, right where we left them. To Dylan's left, the glass window overlooking the park hangs open, as though was trying to escape out onto the rigging when Fliss caught him. I guess the rigging is how he's been moving around the park so fast.

The door clicks shut behind me and I whirl around.

Fliss smiles coldly. "Have you ever had a near-death

experience, Ally?"

Her tone is bitter, overflowing with repressed anger. Suddenly everything clicks into place.

"What's going on? Did you plan this?" I whisper. "Rhona? Maddie? Jazz?"

"Collateral damage." Seeing that I'm preparing to run, Fliss leaps forward, and the next thing I know I'm on my back and her knife is at my throat, point almost piercing my skin.

"And Dylan?" I croak. "I thought … you loved … him."

"I did!"

Fliss's voice is a crazed screech. She's sitting on my chest, pinning me to the floor. I can't breathe. She pushes the blade deeper into my throat, and I feel a sharp sting as it draws blood.

"I loved him, and you knew it! I loved him ever since we were in first grade, but that didn't stop you from swooping in and stealing him from me, Ally, did it?"

"I though t … that was … just a crush. He wasn't … into you …"

"Oh, but he was." Fliss moves her face close to mine. I can smell her sweet breath from the cola she was drinking earlier. "I proved that, didn't I? And yet he still wanted you back. *Still!* You and your fucking love spell!"

I gather all my strength. "The fucking … spell … never

… worked! He … loved … me!"

On the final word, I lift my head—the only part of my body I can move—and crack my forehead into hers. Fliss screams. Drops the knife with a clatter. I'm dizzy, but at least I had warning. I'm the first to recover, and I scrabble for the knife. Close my hand round its hilt. Stab it at the nearest part of Fliss I can reach: her eye.

Fliss drops back with a howl, clutching at her eye. Blood streams between her fingers. I make for the door. I can almost smell freedom.

Then something grabs me round the ankle, and I topple forward. I put my hands out to save myself, narrowly avoiding falling on my own blade. I roll onto my side and see Dylan looming over me. He brings his heavy-booted foot down on my wrist and I scream, letting go of the knife as my bones fracture. My vision goes white with pain, but I come back to myself just in time to see Dylan pick up the knife.

I try to scramble back towards the door, on my butt, leaning on my one good hand.

"Why?" I scream, hoping to stall him somehow. "Why are you doing this?"

"Because I told him to." Behind Dylan, Fliss is back on her feet. I can't see her eye for the blood that's smeared all over her face and hands. "Because he loves me, don't you,

Dylan?"

Dylan doesn't speak. He bears down on me with the knife, but he's moving like an automaton. It's weird. And that's when it hits me.

"The love spell. You did it. You found some way to make it work."

Behind Dylan, Fliss's face contorts into a crazed grin.

"He'll do anything for me, Ally," she says. "Anything." She turns to Dylan. "Kill her. Now."

Dylan lunges for me, and I roll away. Somehow, I manage to get up on my knees, and as he loses his balance, I'm there, flinging myself at him, ignoring the pain in my broken wrist as we both go down. I make the most of his surprise in order to swipe the knife from between his loosened fingers, and I slam it into his throat, again and again and again. Blood spurts everywhere, coating my face, my hands, getting in my eyes, turning my vision red. Dylan lets out a strangled sound, somewhere between a gargle and a howl, but his throat is slashed to pieces. He can't speak or breathe. He grabs at me with a useless hand, fingers tearing at my face, and then falls back to the ground.

I turn to Fliss. I'm still holding the knife. She's backing away. She's scared of me now.

"You're insane," I tell her.

Fliss shakes her head, holding her hands up in a gesture

of surrender. "You … you were going to leave me, Ally. Don't you see?" She gestures towards my wrists. "You were my best friend, and you tried to kill yourself. I was hurt! I didn't want to lose you. I thought we were friends. I thought if we killed Dylan together, you'd see …"

She's babbling now, backing up towards the big window overlooking the park. None of it makes any sense.

"It's us! It's always been us! The spell worked! Look what we can do, together, Ally. The both of us. We could be powerful together. Witches and friends. Forever."

She stops moving. Her backside is pressed against the window frame. Above her waist, the window's open, and behind her is nothing but air. She's trapped, and she knows it.

"This is what you wanted," she tries. One last-ditch attempt to save her own life. "You wanted to die."

All it's going to take is one hard shove.

"No," I say. "I want to live."

I go to push her, but she's too quick. She grabs my wrists, spins me around, and the next thing I know, I'm the one hanging out the window. The rigging's right by me. When Fliss lets go I grab for the rope with my good hand and catch it just before I fall. I clamber up onto the rigging, but Fliss comes after me, crawling out the window, knife in hand. She catches up and we wrestle on the swaying rigging, high above the hall of mirrors.

Have you ever had a near-death experience?

I did. I slit my wrists; I almost died. My life didn't flash before my eyes. I wasn't afraid. I detached from myself. I was eerily calm, and that comes back to me now—the calm. Fliss lunges at me again and I dodge, leaning back, putting my boot in the middle of her chest.

As she falls, I cling to the rigging for dear life.

I want to *live.*

ABOUT THE AUTHOR

Antonia Rachel Ward is horror author and B-movie fan based in Cambridgeshire, UK. Her short stories and poetry have been published in multiple anthologies and her gothic horror novella, *Marionette*, was published by Brigid's Gate Press in August 2022. She is also the founder and editor-in-chief of Ghost Orchid Press.

ALSO BY ANTONIA RACHEL WARD

AVAILABLE FROM BRIGID'S GATE PRESS